"Are you a cop?"

"No." He tugged on his longish hair. "Do I look like a cop?"

"No, but you sound like one."

"Just common sense," he said with a shrug.

She called the local sheriff while J.D. checked the outside of the house with a flashlight. If Zendaris's guys had broken in, they wouldn't leave anything, but a thief looking for a quick fix just might. But would a junkie have left the house in such good order?

He trailed the beam from his flashlight along the window ledges and ground surrounding the house. He couldn't see much in the dark. He'd have to look around tomorrow. He definitely planned to be here tomorrow. And the next day. And the next...

Anything to keep Noelle safe.

CAROL ERICSON

CONCEAL, PROTECT

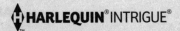

HARLEQUIN® INTRIGUE®

Recycling programs
for this product may
not exist in your area.

ISBN-13: 978-0-373-69682-6

CONCEAL, PROTECT

Printed in U.S.A.

ABOUT THE AUTHOR

Carol Ericson lives with her husband and two sons in Southern California, home of state-of-the-art cosmetic surgery, wild freeway chases, palm trees bending in the Santa Ana winds and a million amazing stories. These stories, along with hordes of virile men and feisty women, clamor for release from Carol's head. It makes for some interesting headaches until she sets them free to fulfill their destinies and her readers' fantasies. To find out more about Carol, her books and her strange headaches, please visit her website, www.carolericson.com, "where romance flirts with danger."

Books by Carol Ericson

CAST OF CHARACTERS

J.D.—Mysterious Prospero Team Three agent who's been assigned the task of keeping close to a woman who might know too much, but as the threats against her escalate, J.D. finds he can't get close enough.

Noelle Dupree—A widow, who witnessed her husband's murder, she's been keeping a tight rein on everything in her life, including her emotions, but when a sexy spy lands on her doorstep, her loss of control might cost her more than she bargained for.

Ted Dupree—Noelle's flaky half brother stumbles onto a plot with international consequences, and this time not even his famous charm may be enough to save him.

Bruce Pierpont III—Noelle's wealthy admirer follows her to Colorado and she knows his intentions aren't completely innocent, but are they sinister?

Abby Warren—Noelle's roommate disappeared suddenly, but she left a web of danger and intrigue behind that seems to be leading Noelle to the same fate as her roommate.

Ally Nettles—Noelle's childhood friend bears a striking resemblance to Noelle...and it just might get her killed.

Nico Zendaris—An international arms dealer who was burned by Prospero Team Three; now he wants revenge and nothing's going to get in his way this time.

Chapter One

The red plastic tray clattered to the floor, and Noelle Dupree jumped as if she'd heard a gunshot. Just like the one that had killed her husband.

She crouched and snatched up the tray with a shaky hand. She was regressing. Loud noises hadn't startled her for at least a year.

She smacked the tray back onto the pile at the beginning of the assembly line, ignoring that she hadn't lined it up with the others, and pursed her lips. She'd done too much work to go back to that quivering mass of nerves she'd become after Alex's murder.

And yet—she looked over her shoulder—she couldn't shake this feeling she'd had over the past few weeks that someone was following her. Watching. Measuring.

Could it be the cops? She'd been the one to call the police when her roommate, Abby, hadn't returned from a business trip. The police had come out to the apartment, questioned her, looked through a few of Abby's things, confiscated Abby's computers and then disappeared.

When she'd called to follow up, the sergeant with the D.C. Metro Police had told her Abby's disappearance was out of their hands. What did that mean?

Her roommate had been private and solitary, and that had suited Noelle perfectly. Now she didn't even have the name of a relative she could contact about Abby. But if the police weren't worried, why should she be worried?

Because someone is following you now.

"What kind of soup would you like, Noelle? We have lentil or chicken noodle today."

She stretched her lips into a smile and peered through the glass, which had fogged up with the steam from the two soups as the server tilted up the lids. "I'll have the chicken noodle tonight, Gary, to go."

She shoved along the food line at the aptly named Spy City Café in the Spy Museum, across from the American Art Museum where she worked. Maybe she should tour the Spy Museum and see if she could pick up a few clues— proof that someone was spying on her and the means to put an end to it.

Tapping on the glass, she said, "Half a turkey sandwich, please."

At the register, the cashier bagged her soup and sandwich and rang up her food. "We're open another hour, Noelle. Sure you don't want to eat in?" The cashier tilted the foam cup back and forth. "Free refills on your drink."

"Not today." Noelle shook back her sleeve and aimed a worried glance at her watch. "It's past five, and I still need to walk a few blocks to catch the Metro."

"Then I'll double bag your soup."

The brisk air needled her cheeks as she hitched her purse crossways over her body while clutching her dinner. She'd changed into tennis shoes in her office at the museum before leaving for the day, and now her rubber soles squished on the damp sidewalk as she strode up Seventh Street toward the Metro station.

A homeless man lounged in the doorway of a building and stuck out his hand as she passed him. She cut a wide berth around the extended hand with its filthy fingernails.

The man snapped his fingers at her. She tripped over a crack in the sidewalk.

He cackled behind her, and she took a quick peek to make sure he hadn't come after her. One of her coworkers had dropped some change in the man's hand once, and he'd rewarded her by grabbing her wrist.

When a threat stared her in the face, she could deal with it. She couldn't handle this vague feeling of being watched.

A rush of people descended the stairs to the Gallery Place–Chinatown Metro station, and Noelle jostled along with them, protecting her soup. The hustle and bustle of people on their way home from work should've eased the tension that she'd allowed to steal through her body over the past few weeks. Her gaze darted among the faces, and the knots in her stomach got tighter.

She slipped onto the train and perched on the edge of a seat next to a woman engrossed in a magazine. Noelle swayed with the motion of the train, her soup sloshing in its container.

When she got to her station, she swiveled her head from side to side to make sure she didn't have a shadow. Then she emerged on the sidewalk and made a beeline for her apartment building.

She punched in the code for the front door and jogged up the one flight of stairs to the apartment she now had all to herself. Her plastic bag of food hung from her wrist as she inserted her key in the dead bolt. The lock turned to the right with no click, and Noelle froze, butterflies fluttering in her belly.

Had she forgotten to lock the dead bolt this morning?

Holding her breath, she tried the door handle, which didn't budge. She shoved the key into the lock and twisted the handle, pushing the door open.

The lamp she left burning all day cast a glow over her living room…and all the upended furniture and tossed drawers.

JARED DOUGLAS CLENCHED his hands into fists inside the white van parked on Noelle Dupree's street. He dipped his chin to speak into the mic clipped to his jacket. "She just walked into her apartment."

A disembodied voice crackled and then filled the van. "What's she doing?"

J.D. peered at the tall, dark-haired woman on the computer monitor in front of him. His gut rolled. "She dropped a bag of what looks like her dinner and flew out of there. Five, four, three, two, one."

Noelle burst out the front door of her apartment building, clutching her cell phone, and J.D. murmured, "Good girl. Get out of there."

Even though J.D. knew the danger had left the building, Noelle's actions showed she had her head on straight. She didn't know that the intruders who had ransacked her place had split two hours ago. For all she knew, they could be lurking in her closet.

Paul's voice intruded on his thoughts. "Did she leave?"

"She's on the sidewalk now, talking on her cell phone." He punched a few keys on the laptop and squinted at the phone number that popped up on the screen. "Calling D.C. Metro."

"Those boys know this place is ours?"

"Lieutenants and above know. The patrol officers are going to check it out just like any other break-in call."

"You don't think they'll find our cameras, do you?" Paul cleared his throat.

"Not a chance." J.D. kept an eye on Noelle in his rear-view mirror as she ended the call and edged closer to the busy bakery two doors down from her building. She'd pocketed her phone and was pacing in front of the bakery window.

She stopped. Her head jerked up. She seemed to be staring at the van.

J.D. slumped farther in his seat and shifted his surveillance of her to the side mirror. That wouldn't look good if a subject made a Prospero agent. Maybe Ms. Noelle Dupree had spent too much time in that Spy Museum.

She straightened her shoulders and took two long, purposeful steps toward the van.

J.D. grabbed the keys swaying from the ignition. The lady had guts, but confronting a would-be thief wasn't the brightest move.

A cop car swung around the corner, stopping Noelle in her tracks. She now aimed her steps at the approaching patrol car, and J.D. released a long breath.

She started talking to the officers before they even got out of their car. She waved her arms and gestured toward her apartment building—and toward him.

One of the cops loped down the sidewalk toward the van, and J.D. dug his wallet out of his pocket. The officer tapped on the window, and J.D. powered it down.

"Sir, what business do you have in this neighborhood?" The beam from the cop's flashlight swept through the van and settled on the laptop in the passenger seat.

J.D. flipped open his ID. "Official business."

The patrol officer peered at the ID and tracked back to J.D.'s face. "Does it have to do with this woman and her ransacked apartment?"

"It does, but we didn't ransack the apartment."

"Got it." He gave a mock salute. "So you just finished a painting job?"

"That's right, Officer." He stuffed his wallet back in his

pocket. "You're not going to find any fingerprints in that apartment or any other type of evidence."

"Didn't think so."

"But make Ms. Dupree feel like you're doing your job. Make her feel safe. And we'll take on that responsibility from here."

"You got it." He strolled away and joined Noelle and the other cop still on the sidewalk.

Noelle turned toward the steps of her apartment building to take the officers up to her place. She rested her foot on the first step and turned to look at the white painting van once more.

From his side mirror, J.D. studied the pale oval of her face framed by dark hair and whispered, "Stay safe, Noelle Dupree."

JACK COBURN'S DARK gaze bored into J.D. over his steepled fingers. "Did our cameras catch the intruders?"

"A couple of Zendaris lackeys. I was too far away to catch them in the act." J.D. shrugged and tipped his chair back on two legs. "I knew they wouldn't find anything in Ms. Dupree's apartment anyway. We'd already gone through her place—only we left it as we found it."

"She hasn't noticed you stalking her?"

"Stalking? Just doing my job, boss." J.D. fought hard to keep the warm flush spreading across his chest from creeping into his face. Coburn didn't miss a thing, and J.D. didn't want to give him any ammunition. Truth was, his surveillance of Noelle, Ms. Dupree, did feel more like a stalking than a tail, especially having those cameras in her apartment.

Not that he'd taken full advantage of that window into her intimate world. He'd allowed her some privacy. Prospero aimed to keep her safe—and to verify she knew nothing of her roommate's secrets—not play a game of Peeping Tom.

But he felt he'd gotten to know her through his observations. He hadn't had one conversation with the woman, and yet he knew of her sadness, her courage, her fears.

Oh, boy. He dragged a hand through his hair. If Coburn could read his thoughts right now, he'd yank him off this case faster than a desert roadrunner.

"Are you sure she hasn't noticed you around?" Coburn leveled a finger at him. "You're kind of hard to miss."

J.D.'s thoughts wandered to the day on the street a few weeks ago when Noelle's gaze had turned toward the van. No way she saw his face that day. He'd had the painter's cap pulled low over his eyes and had kept her in his rearview and side mirrors.

"She never saw me. I'm better than that, Jack."

Coburn's lips twisted into a smile. "Yeah, you're good, J.D. She's on the move, you know."

"Huh?" J.D.'s chair fell forward with a thump. He'd left Noelle for a week and look what happened. "Do you think she knows something about where Abby stashed those plans?"

"She might, but I don't think this move has anything to do with that. She's heading out to Colorado tomorrow."

"To her family's ranch?"

"You *are* good. That's exactly where she's going."

J.D. blew out a breath. "She should be safer there than D.C."

"Are you kidding?" Coburn raised one eyebrow. "You don't think Zendaris will put someone on her, even in Colorado?"

"I'm sure he will, but the ranch sits outside a small town. Anyone Zendaris sends will stick out like a striped cow in the herd."

Coburn shook his head. "You need to stop with the weird similes."

"Similes? We weren't all English lit majors like you, Jack."

"Comparisons. This particular Colorado town has a ski resort. It's winter. It's snowing. Maybe a couple of strangers won't stick out like…whatever."

A chill touched J.D.'s spine. Why had he thought a trip to Colorado would keep Noelle safe? If Zendaris thought she could lead him to those plans he coveted, he'd follow her to the ends of the earth. "They're going to follow her."

"That's right, and so are you."

"More surveillance? I can fit in there. I can ski."

Coburn smacked a file on his desk. "More than surveillance this time, J.D. I want you up close and personal with Ms. Noelle Dupree."

J.D. let a mask of indifference fall over his face as the hard truth smacked him upside the head.

He wanted nothing more than to get up close and personal with Ms. Noelle Dupree.

Chapter Two

Noelle cranked on the old truck and gave it some gas this time. It sputtered and died—again. She pounded the steering wheel, as if that could help.

A tap on the window almost sent her through the roof of the car. She jerked her head to the side and met the tawny eyes of the long, lean cowboy she'd spotted in the grocery store. She'd noticed him cruising the aisles but hadn't gotten the full effect of his gorgeousness.

She powered down the window. "It won't turn over."

"I noticed." He tipped his head toward the hood of the car and a lock of golden-brown hair slipped from beneath his cowboy hat over one eye. "Do you want me to have a look?"

She studied his strong face and the easy smile that relieved it of too much seriousness. He didn't look like a serial killer. "Sure, if you don't mind."

"Don't mind a bit." He parked his grocery cart next to the lamppost and ambled toward the front of her car. He tried the hood and then made a clicking motion with his fingers.

Idiot. She hadn't released the hood. She reached beneath the steering column and yanked on the release lever. The hood popped, and the man thrust it up with a creak.

She could see his hands moving among the innards

of her truck, but not the rest of him. Maybe he was making the situation worse so she'd break down and be at his mercy.

Closing her eyes, she took a deep, cleansing breath of the cold, clear Colorado air. That might have happened in D.C. where strangers stalked you and broke into your apartment and where roommates disappeared without a trace and nobody seemed to care, but she'd relocated, temporarily at least, to laid-back Colorado. Those kinds of things didn't happen here…did they?

He slammed the hood, and she flinched. "Give it a try now."

She turned the ignition and the truck growled to life. Good-looking *and* handy. She poked her head out the window. "Thanks. How'd you do that?"

"You had a loose fuel clip." He wiped his hands on the seat of his jeans. "I tightened it up, but you should have a mechanic check it out so it doesn't happen again. You might need a new fuel pump."

"Thanks again." She chewed her lip. Should she offer him money? Invite him out for coffee? She'd promised herself a fresh start and that meant being open to new relationships instead of hiding in a hole.

He smacked the roof of the car, and she flinched again. "No problem, but get it checked out. Looks like it might snow, and you don't want to be stranded on the road."

She shivered in her jacket. "That's for sure."

The man retrieved his grocery cart and wheeled away with the wave of his hand and a long stride.

She'd missed her opportunity to thank him properly, but maybe he was in town for the skiing and she'd see him again. She could buy him coffee then—even if he had a wife or girlfriend with him because, honestly, that man couldn't possibly be available.

She allowed herself a small smile as she navigated through the parking lot. It had been a long time since she'd wondered about a man's marital status. Dr. Eliason would see it as progress.

The old truck rumbled along the road out of Buck Ridge, along with other vehicles heading away from the ski resort and back to condos and cabins for the night. She hadn't been back to the old homestead in several years, and the activity around the ski resort had surprised her—in a good way.

She'd worried about the loneliness of retreating to the empty ranch house. Her father had died years ago, and Mom, frail and increasingly plagued by her obsessive-compulsive disorder, had moved in with Aunt Kathy down in Scottsdale.

And her brother, Ted? No telling where he'd been holing up for the past few years.

So the ranch had fallen to her. There'd been a time when she and Alex had planned to live at the ranch and paint and sculpt and sell their stuff to tourists.

Tears blurred her vision, and she wiped the back of her hand across her nose. Even if some thief hadn't murdered her husband, Noelle knew they would've never made it to their golden years together.

That had made Alex's death even harder to deal with—the guilt.

The truck hiccuped a few times on the way back to the ranch, but the cowboy had done a good job.

She passed the entrance to the Bar N Ranch, and on a whim, made a U-turn at the next turnout. Her friend Tara Nettles had moved back home a few years ago after her divorce. They'd run into each other on Noelle's first day back in town and had lunch, and Tara had told her to drop by anytime.

The truck churned up dirt on the road to the house. Too bad the cowboy wasn't here to make sure the truck started again when it was time to leave.

Tara must've seen her coming because she was heading down the front steps before Noelle even stopped the truck. Noelle slid from the front seat and hopped to the ground.

"You said anytime, and I was passing by. Do you want me to come back another time?"

Tara flipped her long black hair over her shoulder. "Perfect timing. I just took some cookies out of the oven."

"I can smell them from here." Noelle sniffed the sweet scent of vanilla on the air. "Didn't take you for the baking kind, Tara."

"I'm a regular prairie home companion out here even though we have mountains instead." She rolled her eyes. "Come on in. Mom's been anxious to see you ever since I told her we had lunch."

Tara took her by the arm and led her up the porch steps. "Ma, look who dropped by."

Noelle followed Tara into the kitchen, cheerful with its yellow walls and blue-and-yellow chintz curtains. Mrs. Nettles sat at the kitchen table, cradling a cup of something hot. She lowered her glasses to her nose. "Noelle Dupree. You still look just like my Tara."

"Don't get up." Noelle bent over the older woman and kissed the papery skin of her cheek. "You look great."

Mrs. Nettles waved her hands. "I look like hell. Hasn't your mother told you that growing old isn't for sissies?"

"Something like that."

"Of course, neither is life." Mrs. Nettles tilted her head. "Tara told me what happened to your husband, dear. What a tragedy."

"Yes, it was." Noelle blinked. Mrs. Nettles didn't know that the real tragedy was that Noelle hadn't loved her husband enough. Maybe if she had that whole night would've turned out differently.

"Cookies?" Tara held up a plate piled high with lumpy rounds.

Noelle wrinkled her nose. "What I said before about you not being the baking kind? It doesn't look like you are."

"These?" Tara thrust the plate at her. "They may not look perfect, but they're yummy. Right, Ma?"

"They're oatmeal, chocolate chip." Mrs. Nettles shrugged her thin shoulders. "She thinks everything tastes better with a few chocolate chips thrown in."

"I agree." Noelle reached for a cookie and took a bite. "Mmm, perfection."

"Told you." Tara pulled out a chair. "Have a seat. Do you want some coffee?"

"I can't stay long. I have groceries in the car."

Tara tugged her sweater around her body. "Nothing's going to spoil in this weather."

"So how does small-town life compare to Chicago?" Noelle licked some chocolate from her fingers. When Tara and her husband had divorced, she'd left him in Chicago and returned home to take care of her mother. And apparently take up baking.

"Of course, it's a lot slower, but the popularity of that ski resort has changed things up a bit from when we were kids. People lock their doors now, for one thing."

"Crime in Buck Ridge?"

"Mostly around the resort. Like any ski resort, it attracts drifters and partiers and scammers."

And which category fit the cowboy?

"Then how much longer before Buck Ridge lures that brother of yours back here?" Mrs. Nettles wagged her finger.

"Half brother," Noelle answered automatically.

"Don't worry, Ma." Tara dragged a finger along the inside of the mixing bowl and popped some cookie dough into her mouth. "I don't have the hots for Teddy Dupree anymore."

Mrs. Nettles eyed her daughter over the top of her glasses. "I should hope not. One bad relationship in a woman's life is enough. Look at Noelle and that sweet boy. That marriage would've lasted a lifetime."

"Maybe Noelle doesn't want to talk about Alex, Ma." Tara mouthed *sorry* to Noelle behind a cupped hand.

"It did last a lifetime—his." Noelle pushed off the counter. "I'd better get those groceries home. Goodbye, Mrs. Nettles."

Tara trailed her to the door and slipped out onto the porch with her. "Sorry about my mother. She thinks everyone's relationships are better than mine."

"They're not. Alex and I—"

Tara held up her hands. "You don't have to explain anything to me. What happened to Alex…and you was horrible. Whatever your relationship was, it shouldn't have ended like that."

Noelle puffed a few breaths into the cold night. "I'll let your mom believe in fairy tales."

Tara gave her a quick hug and watched her walk to the truck. "Are you going to drive that old thing around while you're here or get something else?"

"The truck's okay. I'm not going to be here long enough to buy another car—just a month or two."

"Yeah, that's what I thought. Drive carefully. It got dark while you were inside, but at least the snow hasn't come in yet."

Noelle waved and climbed into the truck. Holding her breath, she turned the key. The engine turned over with a rattle, but it did turn over. That cowboy knew his stuff.

She eased the truck back up the dirt road and turned onto the two-lane highway. It was more deserted now, but still several headlights from town caught up with her and followed her along the highway.

She signaled well in advance before aiming the truck between the posts that marked the entrance to the ranch. Her ranch. When Mom had moved in with her sister, she'd signed the property over to Noelle.

No reason for her mom to leave anything to Ted, since Noelle's half brother wasn't her mother's blood. Dad could've provided for his son before he had died, but he had figured Ted would gamble it, drink it or drug it all away.

Probably figured right, but that didn't stop Noelle from feeling bad that their father hadn't left anything to Ted. Her mother had probably had a hand in that decision.

Noelle had left a light on in the house, but not the porch light since she hadn't planned to stay out after dark. She swung the truck in front of the house, illuminating it with her headlights.

Cutting the engine, she left the headlights on so she wouldn't kill herself going up those rickety steps. The moon had disappeared behind leaden clouds that threatened snow.

She lifted one bag of groceries from the back of the truck and picked her way across the dirt and gravel that littered the path to the front door. She set the bag on the porch and fumbled for her keys.

She unlocked the door and pushed it open, stooping to scoop up the grocery bag on her way in. Two steps into the room and she stopped. The smell. Cologne. Men's cologne. The same cologne favored by her late husband.

Squishing the bag against her chest, she glanced around the living room. Her gaze darted from the magazines she'd stacked on the coffee table, now askew, to the sweatshirt she'd hung by its hood on the doorknob of the closet. It now hung by the back collar.

Panic pumped into her system, and she released her breath in short spurts.

Not again.

Clutching the bag, she spun around and made a beeline for the front door, which still gaped open. When the cold air hit her face, she dropped the bag and stumbled over it.

The headlights blinded her now, and she held her hands in front of her, clawing her way back to the truck and safety.

Until she collided with a body.

Chapter Three

Noelle flew down the front steps and hit his chest. J.D. staggered back, wrapping his arms around her soft body.

She arched her back, drove her heel against the tip of his boot and raised her hands as if to claw his face.

"Whoa, whoa." He crushed her against his frame with one arm and cinched both of her wrists with his other hand. "What's wrong? It's me—the guy who fixed your car."

Her fingers relaxed, but she continued to struggle against him. "Let me go!"

"Are you sure?" With her flailing limbs and rigid muscles, she wouldn't be able to stand on her own two feet.

"Let me go!" This time her voice had a distinct growl around the edges.

He released her, and, as he'd predicted, she stumbled to the ground. Her eyes, iridescent in the glare of the truck's headlights, glowed at him as if they belonged to some fierce creature of the night.

Stepping in front of the truck to block the blinding lights, he stuck out his hand. "Are you okay? Why did you attack me?"

She eyed him over her bent knees, the heels of her hands digging into the ground behind her. "I didn't attack you. What are you doing here?"

"Just wanted to make sure you made it home okay."

That had a false ring to it, since Noelle had stopped at the ranch down the road on her way home. He kept his hand extended in case she changed her mind.

"I did, but…" She cranked her head over her shoulder and looked at the house, the open door behind the screen door, a soft light filtering through the mesh.

J.D.'s pulse picked up speed. Noelle hadn't been running at him but rather away from something in the house. He hooked a hand beneath her arm and nudged her. "What's wrong?"

She allowed him to pull her to her feet. Still gazing at the house, she brushed the dirt from her jeans. "I—I think someone broke into my house."

Damn. Had Zendaris's men followed her already? They must be confident she knew something about the plans or had them in her possession. Zendaris grew bolder by the week.

"You *think?*"

"I put things in a certain order." She folded her arms across her chest and hunched her shoulders. "Someone changed that order. I could tell someone had been in there."

"Do you know for a fact that someone is gone?" He put his hands on his hips, his fingers resting on the weapon secured in his gun bag.

Her eyes widened. "No. I noticed the items out of order and took off."

"Smart thing to do." But then, she'd had practice at that sort of thing. He unzipped his gun bag and withdrew his weapon. "I'm going to check it out."

"Do you know how to use that thing?" She pointed to the gun clutched in his hand.

You have no idea, darlin'. "I've had a little practice. Do you want to wait on the porch or come inside with me?"

"I'll come with you."

He opened the screen door and the bottom hinge fell off the doorjamb.

Noelle, who'd been close behind him, jumped, bumping against his back. "I must've caused that when I flung open the door."

"We'll deal with that later." He rested the bottom corner of the screen door on the porch, an idea forming in his head about a way to get close to Noelle without arousing her suspicion—because she had a lot of suspicions.

He stepped over the threshold, his gun leading the way, and surveyed the front room. He saw no glaring evidence of a break-in. Noelle must be more skittish than an unbroken pony.

"How do you know someone was here?" He lowered his weapon. No need to get trigger-happy.

"The smell hit me first." She took a deep breath, her nostrils flaring. "Men's cologne. I—I recognize the scent, but I haven't had anyone over wearing that. I haven't had anyone over at all."

J.D. sniffed the air, but the only smell filling his nostrils was the freshness of Noelle—light, floral—definitely not a guy's scent. "If you say so."

Her startling blue eyes glared at him. "There are other things." She jerked her thumb over her shoulder. "Do you see those magazines? I had them stacked a certain way. Someone moved them."

He knew from his surveillance of her D.C. apartment that she was religiously neat, but he found it hard to believe she'd remember which way she'd stacked her magazines. "Do you have a pet? A cat?"

"No." She narrowed her eyes, resembling the cat she didn't have. "And even if I did, I don't think the cat could knock that sweatshirt off the closet door handle and then hang it up a different way."

He raised his eyebrows. Was she really that meticulous or had she been setting a trap? Someone this organized would never be able to put up with his habits—not that Noelle Dupree had to put up with anything from him.

"Anything else?" He swung his gun in front of him again. The lady seemed to know what she was talking about, and any hopes he'd had that she'd overreacted and Zendaris really wasn't on her tail just grew dimmer.

"I didn't stay to find out." She waved her arms in front of her, encompassing the room. "I thought we came in here to surprise the intruder."

"I doubt we'd be surprising him now, but let's take a look."

She guided him through the house, where she pointed out other discrepancies between the placement of certain items now and how she'd left them.

Zendaris's thugs had tried to conceal their intrusion this time, unlike their break-in of her apartment in D.C. Why? Probably didn't want to spook her and send her running to some other location. Wanted to take her by surprise this time.

In the bathroom, Noelle flung open the medicine cabinet and gasped.

"What's wrong? Something missing?"

"A bottle of prescription medication." She tapped one glass shelf. "It was right here."

Was it a cover? Had Zendaris's people taken some drugs just in case Noelle noticed the break-in?

"That could be your explanation right there. Are you sure you had the bottle there?"

"Positive."

He believed her. All the bottles in the medicine cabinet were lined up, labels outward.

When they returned to the living room, she perched on

a stool at the counter that separated the kitchen from the living room, and he sat on the arm of an overstuffed chair.

"At least they didn't stick around. I don't get it…." She pursed her lips and dropped her gaze to her hands folded on the counter.

"You don't get what?" Would she open up to him about the break-in in D.C.? It would go a long way to proving to his superiors in Prospero that she knew nothing about her roommate's secret life.

She shook her head. "Buck Ridge used to be such a safe community. My friend was just telling me about the jump in crime since the ski resort took off."

"The price you pay for prosperity." He shrugged. Noelle Dupree didn't open up to just anybody. He'd have to become somebody.

Her long black ponytail swung over her shoulder as she tilted her head at him. "How did you know where I lived?"

"Despite the popularity of the ski resort, Buck Ridge is still a small town. Someone noticed us in the parking lot and told me your name and that you had a ranch out this way. When I saw the name of the ranch from the road, I pulled in to see how you…the truck was doing."

"Really?" She gripped the edge of the tiled island. "That's kind of scary when you think about it."

"That's a small town for you. It was the same where I grew up." He waited for the questions, but they never materialized on her lips. She didn't want to dig too deeply into his life in case he required the same from her.

She hit her forehead with the heel of her hand. "I forgot I still have groceries in the car."

"And your headlights are still on. You don't need a dead battery on top of everything else." He reached around her and swept the keys to the truck from the counter and dangled them in front of her. "You turn your lights off, and I'll get the groceries for you."

"Deal." She snatched the keys from his hand. "You have the advantage over me, you know."

"Huh?" Had he blown his cover already?

"You know my name, but I don't know yours."

"J.D." He left it at that. Two could play at that game.

He carried in all the groceries and parked on a stool while Noelle put away the items. He studied her face, tight with worry.

"Do you have any idea who could've broken into your place? Any local druggies? How's the teenage population around here? Is there much of a problem with narcotics?"

She lined up some cans on a shelf in the pantry and turned them all so the labels faced outward, just like the bottles in the medicine cabinet. "I have no idea."

He expelled a long breath, his chest and his hopes deflating. She had no intention of confiding in him. "Do you want to call the cops?"

Her blue eyes darkened as they darted around the room. "I suppose I should."

"If these *are* druggies, I'm sure the local cops would want to know. Maybe they've hit other people. Maybe there's a pattern and the cops already have some suspects."

"Are *you* a cop?"

"No." He tugged on his longish hair. "Do I look like a cop?"

"No, but you sound like one."

He said with a shrug, "Just common sense."

She called the local sheriff while J.D. checked the outside of the house with a flashlight. If Zendaris's guys had broken in, they wouldn't leave any evidence behind, but a thief looking for a quick fix just might. But would a junkie have left the house in such good order?

He trailed the beam from his flashlight along the window ledges and ground surrounding the house. He couldn't see much in the dark. He'd have to look around tomorrow. He definitely planned to be here tomorrow. And the next day. And the next.

The sheriff's squad car pulled through the broken gates of Noelle's ranch. J.D. added those gates to his growing list of items that needed fixing.

The sheriff stepped out of his car and aimed his flashlight at J.D. "You the fellow with Noelle Dupree?"

Noelle had left the front door open and now edged onto the porch, folding her jacket around her body. "Hey, Sheriff Greavy. This is J.D. He came by just after I discovered the break-in."

He and the sheriff shook hands, and J.D. followed him up the porch.

Sheriff Greavy stepped into the living room and tipped his cowboy hat from his head. "Did you discover anything missing besides the medication, Noelle?"

"My mom left this place pretty sparse, Sheriff. She even took the TV with her to Aunt Kathy's"

"What about your personal belongings? Jewelry? Computer? Camera?"

"I don't have any of that stuff here. I had my laptop with me in the truck." She looked around the room. "And it's still there."

Greavy flipped open a notebook and felt in his pocket for a pen. He found one and opened it against his chin. "You told Marlene that some prescription medication was stolen, but you didn't tell her what kind. What was it?"

Noelle knotted her hands across her waist, while a rosy flush crept into her cheeks. "It was a generic brand of Valium."

After what she'd been through the past month, hell,

the past two years, she didn't have any reason to be embarrassed about using a tranquilizer for stress or anxiety.

The sheriff scribbled a few notes and shoved the notebook back in his pocket. "You doing okay, Noelle? We all heard about—" he shot a glance at J.D. "—your troubles."

Sheriff Greavy didn't have to tiptoe around him. Prospero had already done a full background on Noelle Dupree and knew all about the murder of her husband two years ago.

But Noelle didn't know that, and, judging by the way the color in her cheeks flared up even more, she had no intention of telling him anything about her past.

"I'm fine, Sheriff." She untangled her fingers and shoved her hands in her pockets. "I don't even take that medication. I just have it for insurance."

Sheriff Greavy held up his calloused hands. "No need to explain anything to me, Noelle. Hell, it's better than hitting the bottle when times get tough."

The sheriff asked her a few more questions, dusted the door for fingerprints and then clapped his hat back on his head. "This doesn't surprise me a bit. We've had plenty of break-ins with people stealing TVs, cameras, computers and prescription meds. I don't think it's an organized ring, but at least your burglar was neater than most."

"Yeah, at least he didn't trash the place." She bit her lip, her eyes clouding over.

Must be thinking about that other break-in.

"I have to ask you something, Noelle." Sheriff Greavy paused at the front door, grasping the doorjamb with a gloved hand. "You heard from Teddy?"

"No." Her face had closed up tighter than a bear trap.

"Well, I heard he's back in town." The sheriff jerked his chin toward the room. "You don't think…?"

"No."

"Just askin'. You take care and get a good, solid lock on this door." He touched a finger to the rim of his hat. "J.D."

Noelle didn't have to worry about keeping her brother a secret from him either. Prospero knew all about him, too.

Noelle stood beside him on the porch, watching Sheriff Greavy pull away. Her body vibrated like a taut string that hadn't been plucked in years. If anything, the sheriff's visit had made her more tense.

Seemed as if nothing but land mines filled her past, one incident after another that had to be avoided at all costs.

And she was facing the biggest land mine of all and didn't even know it.

She puffed out a breath, and it hung suspended for a moment in the cold night air. "That wasn't much help."

"I don't know." He stood sideways across the threshold and waved her into the house. As she brushed past him, her ponytail tickled his arm. "Sheriff Greavy has a record of the break-in. That's a good thing."

Pivoting, she faced him, crossing her arms. "Thanks for your help tonight. I mean, for the truck and sticking around after the break-in."

"No problem. Call the garage about getting that truck fixed, and…" Was it too soon to offer his services? Her stance, back ramrod straight and arms folded, screamed *get the hell out.* Probably not the best time.

"And take care. Like Greavy suggested, get a dead bolt on that door."

"Will do."

J.D. ambled toward the door, and she uprooted herself to make sure he made it outside. They said their goodbyes, and she didn't even wait for him to reach his truck before shutting the door.

He slid into his truck and cranked on the heater. Rubbing his hands together and blowing on them, he watched the lights go off in the house until just the yellow glow from the front windows remained.

He backed up and then swung wide to face the dilapidated gates. He pulled onto the deserted road. With his arm draped across the backseat, he backed up until he had a clear view of the entrance to Noelle's ranch.

If Zendaris's men had broken into Noelle's house with her gone, what was stopping them from breaking in with her home? When would looking through her stuff cease to satisfy them? When would they make a move on her?

J.D. slumped in his seat and tipped his hat over his eyes, eyes that saw everything.

He turned the key in the ignition and fiddled with the static radio stations until a woman's dulcet tones flooded the truck. *Ah, a radio therapist dispensing advice to the lovelorn.*

Not that he needed any advice. You had to have a love life to need advice. His fiancée had left him for being too married to his job, and she must've been right because he barely missed her absence.

Jack Coburn had warned them that working for Prospero and having a personal life could be mutually exclusive. Although Jack had managed—he and Lola had an adopted son and Lola was expecting a daughter.

J.D.'s Prospero Team Three buddy, Cade Stark, was currently living below the radar in Europe with his wife and son after Nico Zendaris had threatened their lives.

He pinched the bridge of his nose and yawned. Nobody said this life was gonna be easy.

The side mirror glinted, and J.D. sat up to scan the road from his rearview mirror, cracking open his window. A single headlight pierced the darkness. As it drew closer, the sound of a motorcycle engine whined in the night.

He narrowed his eyes, every muscle tense. The bike

slowed at the dip in the road right before the entrance to Noelle's ranch. When he came up the rise, the rider pulled the bike to the side of the road and cut the engine.

J.D.'s pulse quickened. The motorcycle rider hadn't noticed his truck, nestled up against the bushes across the road from the ranch. Of if he had, he didn't give J.D. a second look.

With his helmet still on his head, the rider hopped off the bike, grabbed the handlebars and pushed the silent motorcycle through Noelle's broken gates.

J.D. didn't know what this guy planned to do at Noelle's place, but his job compelled him to find out and put a stop to it.

His job and the insane attraction he felt for the attractive, reserved widow.

Chapter Four

Noelle flipped open her book at the folded-over page and curled her feet beneath her. The words blurred in front of her. She blinked a few times and then tossed the paperback on the cushion next to her.

That J.D. had impeccable timing. Impeccable muscles, too. She'd even felt them through his jacket when she'd thrown herself into his arms. After the scare of finding the disordered items in the house, those arms had been a welcome refuge.

Alex had never made her feel safe, up to and including the night he was murdered.

She bit her lip as if that could stop the traitorous thought.

Creak. Creak.

Noelle froze, her bottom lip still caught between her teeth. Her gaze darted toward the front door. Someone was on the porch.

She half rose from the couch, her hands clutching the folds of her robe. When Sheriff Greavy and then J.D. had left, she'd pulled her dad's shotgun from the closet and loaded it. It rested against the wall by the front door.

Time to see if it still worked.

She scooted from the couch and tiptoed to the door.

A man shouted, and she grabbed the gun. A scuffling sound replaced the creaking and something or someone crashed into the front door, shaking it on its rotting hinges. More shouting. And cursing.

Another man yelled and the door reverberated with his pounding. "Noelle! Noelle! There's a crazy dude out here."

She hitched the shotgun under her arm and threw open the door.

Her half brother, Ted, blood spouting from his nose, stretched across the porch, his fists poised for another assault on her front door.

Beyond the crumpled mess of her brother, J.D. loomed, hands bunched and a coil to his body that looked ready to spring.

"Stop!" Noelle held up her own hands. "This is my brother, Ted."

Her words did nothing to cut through the ferocity coming off J.D.'s tense frame in solid waves. What had happened to the easygoing cowboy?

Brushing past Ted, she stepped between the two men. "Really. This is my brother. He's harmless—well, sort of."

Ted gasped and gurgled behind her. "Can I get some help here? Dude broke my nose."

J.D. flexed his fingers, and Noelle noticed a smear of blood on one knuckle.

She shuffled forward and stopped, still wary of the danger glittering in his hooded eyes—even though that danger wasn't directed at her. "Did you hurt your hand?"

"Yeah, he hurt his hand—on my nose," Ted wailed and stumbled into the house.

Noelle held J.D.'s gaze, feeling drawn to this man who had gone to battle for her. It had been a long time since someone had been there to protect her.

Bit by bit, J.D. came down from the ledge. He flexed his fingers again. Blinked. Rotated his shoulders. Puffed out a breath.

"It's nothing." He rubbed his knuckles against the thigh of his jeans and tipped his chin toward the open door. "Sorry about your brother."

My brother.

As if coming out of a trance, she covered her mouth with her hand and spun around. "Ted!"

"About damn time." Ted shot her an accusing glance over the hand clapped over his bleeding nose.

"I'll get you some paper towels and ice."

J.D. had followed her into the house and approached Ted, who held up one hand. "Stay away from me."

"Sorry, man. I thought you were an intruder. Someone broke into your sister's house earlier."

"It wasn't me."

Noelle pulled open the freezer door and scooped some ice into a bowl. Did J.D. think it odd that her brother had to make that denial?

"Didn't say it was. Sit."

As Noelle carried the ice into the living room, Ted sank to the edge of the couch. She crouched beside him and handed him a wet paper towel. "Clean up the blood first, wrap this paper towel around some ice and put it on the bridge of your nose."

Ted dragged the paper towel across his nose, keeping an eye on J.D. hovering behind her. "So what did they steal? The people who broke in, I mean?"

"Some prescription meds."

His eyes widened. "Wasn't me." His gaze shifted to J.D. "I'm clean, have been for seven months."

"Congratulations. Weird coincidence, though—someone breaks in, steals some drugs and then you show up."

"Would I show up if I'd just stolen from you?" He tossed a bloody lump of paper towel on the coffee table.

"Pick that up." She wrinkled her nose. "I never know what you're up to, Ted."

"Not stealing from my sister."

"Not anymore?"

"Okay, okay." He pointed past her shoulder. "Who's this guy, anyway?"

"This is J.D...." She trailed off. Had he ever given her a last name? "J.D., this is my brother, Ted."

J.D. shoved his hands in his pockets and eyed Ted's bloodstained hands. "Don't take it the wrong way that I don't want to shake your hand."

"Hey, what's a handshake when you already busted my nose?"

"It's not broken."

Ted peeled the soggy paper towel from his face. "How do you know?"

J.D. shrugged. "I didn't hear it crack when I punched you."

Pinching his nose again, Ted said in a nasal voice, "Are you a friend of Noelle's or her watchdog?"

"A little of both, I guess." He raised one brow at Noelle, and her insides turned squishy.

"H-how's your hand? Is it still bleeding?"

J.D. inspected his knuckles. "Never was. That was Ted's blood."

Ted snorted and then coughed.

"Ted, do you want some water? Something stronger?" She half turned toward the kitchen. She had to keep busy around J.D. or she'd end up staring into his whiskey-colored eyes and falling into a trance again.

"I told you. I'm on the wagon."

"Booze, too?"

"If you get off one, you have to get off the other. That's what my sponsor told me, anyway, and he has a point."

"I'm glad you're taking this seriously. Water, then?"

"Or a soda—anything with caffeine." He shrugged. "I can't give up all my vices at once." He tapped a hard carton in his front pocket. "Back on the cigs, too."

"Not in the house." She crossed one index finger over the other. "I have some cola. J.D.?"

"Just some water."

She moved toward the kitchen and then tripped on the leg of a barstool as a thought that had been niggling the edges of her mind slammed full force into her brain.

She gripped the edge of the counter and turned. "What were you doing out there, anyway, J.D.? You'd left almost a half hour before."

He sauntered toward the kitchen and parked on the edge of a barstool. "Since I was out this way anyway, I drove up the road to have a look at a place for rent. On my way back to town, I saw your brother walking his motorcycle onto your property. After what happened earlier—" he spread his hands "—I thought I'd check it out."

Noelle released her breath in short wisps, so J.D. wouldn't realize she'd been holding it waiting for his answer.

Sounded plausible. Or he was a great liar.

"Checking it out is one thing. Tackling a guy and pummeling the life out of him is something else." Ted lifted the ice from his nose to aim a scowl at J.D.

"Your actions were suspicious. Why didn't you just walk up to the door and knock? Why were you creeping up the porch and peering through the window like some sort of Peeping Tom?"

Ted placed the ice pack back on his face and answered in a muffled voice, "Just wanted to make sure Noelle was here. I'd heard you were back in town, sis. Wanted to see if it was really you first."

"Who else would be here?" She slid a glass of water

toward J.D. and rolled her eyes. Then she clinked the can of soda on the coffee table in front of Ted.

"How the hell would I know? You don't keep me apprised of *your* property."

Noelle pressed her lips together. *It could've been your property, too, bro, if you hadn't traveled a path of drug addiction, gambling and petty crime.* At least that's what she'd told herself over the years. Maybe she should have shared the ranch with him.

"Sounds like someone's keeping you apprised since you came out here to see me." She folded her arms and wedged a hip against the kitchen island. "Spill."

Ted buried his face farther into the ice pack. "I still have a few connections here. Word gets out."

"Tara? Have you been in touch with Tara?"

"Now and again."

"Her mom's going to be real happy about that."

"Maybe she will. I've changed, Noelle."

"Actions speak louder than words. What are you doing back in Buck Ridge? Are you planning to stay here at the ranch?"

J.D. knocked over his water glass, and the clear liquid spread across the tile. "Oops. I'll get that."

He hoisted his tall, rangy frame off the stool and swiped a kitchen cloth from the oven door handle.

Ted dropped the ice pack from his face and straightened his shoulders. "I was hoping I could stay here or even in the guesthouse. I'll get a job and pay some rent, of course."

"Of course."

"Or…I could do some work around the ranch in exchange for room and board. God knows, the old place could use some sprucing up."

Bam. Noelle knew that was coming. Ted would camp out here free of charge, eating, hanging around the house and not doing one lick of work. In fact, the *old place* would end up looking a lot worse than it did now.

Her gaze settled on J.D.'s strong hands mopping up the water on the counter. She sucked in her bottom lip and raised her eyes to his. She gave him a wink.

"That's not necessary, Ted. J.D.'s going to stay in the guesthouse in exchange for sprucing up the ranch."

J.D.'S HAND ALMOST slid off the counter. Getting close to Noelle Dupree had been easier than he'd expected. He'd figured he'd have an uphill battle, and here she was inviting him to stay with her.

Her brother—*half* brother—looked him over from head to toe with his shifty eyes. His and Noelle's eyes obviously didn't share the same half. J.D. could get lost in Noelle's deep blue, almost-violet eyes. Dreamy. Soulful. Her half brother's brown eyes had a hard edge. They measured, assessed.

J.D. didn't completely believe Ted didn't have a hand in the break-in. He'd like to believe that instead of the alternative, anyway. Something about the guy was off. J.D. had taken him for a thief the minute he'd seen him skulking around Noelle's porch.

Noelle nudged him with her foot, and he swept the dishcloth from the counter and tossed it into the sink. "That's right. Noelle hired me on today. I'm moving into the guesthouse tomorrow."

Hell, he hadn't even known this ranch *had* a guesthouse.

Ted narrowed his eyes. "Weren't you just looking at a place to rent up the road?"

The guy might be a former druggie, but he didn't miss a thing. "For a friend."

"Right." Ted pushed off the couch, gathering the bloody paper towels in his hands. "My other offer still stands,

Noelle. I can get a job at the ski resort and pay you rent in exchange for a room in the house…maybe even my old room."

She snorted. "Come off it, Ted. You never really had a room here. You lived with your mom in Buck Ridge most of the time."

He dumped the paper towels in the trash can. "Will you consider it?"

"Get the job first."

"I will. I'm good for it, Noelle. I'm a changed man."

"Glad to hear it. Do you have a place to stay tonight?"

Ted smiled, the charming smile of a con man. J.D. could recognize it a mile away. "You're not so hard after all. I thought that thing with Alex had changed you, turned you into your mother. But maybe you're getting back to the sweet girl I grew up with."

Noelle's chin jutted forward. "You mean the one you scammed all the time?"

"Aw, I wouldn't put it like that." Ted shrugged into his well-worn jacket. "Anyway, as luck would have it, I do have a place to crash tonight and for the next few nights. But I'd like to stay in my family home." He held up his hands as Noelle opened her mouth. "I'll get that job first, sis."

She snapped her mouth shut and nodded. "You get that job, and we'll talk."

She walked Ted to the door, and he gave her a hug, which she returned with one arm. He waved to J.D. "No hard feelings, man. I probably would've done the same thing in your place."

"Yeah, sorry about your nose. It'll be okay."

This time, Ted didn't walk his bike off the ranch silently. The engine roared to life and he fishtailed down the drive, stirring up a cloud of dust.

Noelle sighed beside him. "You must think I'm a terrible sister, but the family put up with a lot from Ted. He's had his share of problems—most of them self-induced."

"I know the type, and I think you handled it great. You're no enabler."

"Not anymore." She folded her hands behind her and leaned against the doorjamb. "About our deal."

"Uh-huh?" His gaze dropped to her mouth and he dragged his attention back to her eyes, which darkened to a violet hue.

"I just said that so I didn't have to offer the guesthouse to Ted. You don't really have to work on the ranch in exchange for room and board, but thanks for playing along."

"I wasn't playing."

"What?"

He had her right where he wanted her, or at least had himself right where he wanted to be.

"I wasn't playing any game, Noelle."

"What do you mean? I wasn't really making you that offer. I just came up with it at the spur of the moment to get Teddy off my back."

He took one step closer to her, close enough to inhale her fresh scent. "But you made the offer—in front of a witness—and I'm taking it. I'm moving into your guesthouse, Noelle Dupree."

Chapter Five

Noelle gulped. Did he just say he was taking her up on her offer? She couldn't think straight with him standing so close, those tawny eyes staring deep into hers. The clean, outdoorsy smell of him clouding her senses.

He must've misunderstood. "No, really. I don't need any help with the ranch. It was just a way to get rid of Ted."

He lifted the sagging screen door with two fingers and let it drop. "You don't need help with the ranch?"

"I never meant—"

He put a finger to her lips, and she had to clutch the doorknob behind her.

"I know you said it to get rid of your brother, but it sounds like he's going to stick around. Buck Ridge is a small town. How are you going to explain the fact that I'm not staying in the guesthouse and helping out?"

Thankfully, he removed his finger from her lips and she could breathe again—and even talk. "I'll cross that bridge when I come to it."

"I like your suggestion. I need a place to stay, I'm familiar with ranches, I'm handy and it will keep away that brother of yours."

She *did* need help with the ranch. She'd come here to make some improvements and see if she could maybe turn that guesthouse into a studio.

And she had to admit, J.D.'s presence would be a comfort. Her gaze roamed over his lean, muscled frame, and she swallowed. Maybe *comfort* wasn't the right word. Security. Safety. She looked into his eyes. Danger.

She could use a little more of that kind of danger in her life. "The guesthouse isn't much. It has a bathroom with a shower but no kitchen."

"I'm not much of a cook, anyway. And you don't have to pay me. The room is enough."

She shoved at the screen door with her toe. "This place needs a lot of work. I'll pay you a salary, and you'll earn it."

"Deal." He stuck out his hand. They were standing so close, his fingers brushed her arm.

They shook on it, and Noelle had to snatch her hand back or fall victim to the magnetism between them and never let go. She had to plant her feet back on the ground. "I don't even know your last name."

"Davis. Jim Davis. Everyone calls me J.D."

"Where are you from, J.D.? What are you doing in Buck Ridge?" If she kept up the interrogation, she could ignore these other feelings swirling in her head—feelings traitorous to Alex.

"I'm from Texas. I grew up on a ranch. I was recently discharged from the service. Just trying to figure out what I want to do with my life."

Military. She could see that. Polite. Stand-up guy. And he had no problem jumping into dangerous situations. He'd be handy to have around in more ways than one.

"Working on a run-down ranch is what you want to do with your life?"

"Not with my life, but right now, it works for me, and it works for you, too."

"I suppose you want to go back to your hotel and come back tomorrow with your stuff. Or is tomorrow too soon?"

She sealed her lips together. Didn't want to seem too eager to have him here.

"If you don't mind, I'd rather check it out now and stay there tonight. I'll get my stuff tomorrow."

She pressed her back against the door. Could she trust this man? She knew next to nothing about him and yet he'd come to her rescue twice already. Did chivalry motivate him or something else?

Releasing a breath, she ducked around him and snagged the key to the guesthouse from the hook in the kitchen.

"Your castle awaits."

"Castle?" He lifted an eyebrow in her direction, oblivious that she'd already been thinking of him as a chivalrous knight.

"Maybe I exaggerated. It needs some work, but everything in the bathroom is in working order and it's furnished."

"As long as there's a bed."

She dropped the key she'd been juggling between her hands and bent over to retrieve it, hiding her warm cheeks in the process. The idea of this man in bed—any bed—lit a fuse under some wicked thoughts that had been dormant for too long.

As her fingers groped for the key chain on the dark porch, J.D. crouched beside her, sweeping his hand across the back of hers.

"Here they are." He held them up, and they jingled between them. "Do you have a flashlight? I think we're going to need one if we hope to make it to the guesthouse without tripping over each other."

She popped up and spun back toward the house, eager to escape his overwhelming presence and the guilt she felt every time the electric current zapped between them.

"I have a flashlight in the closet. I don't know how I thought we'd get out there without one."

She stumbled back into the house and grabbed a flashlight from the closet shelf. When she got out to the porch, she shined the light on J.D., leaning against a sagging wood post, tossing the keys in the air and whistling.

But he didn't fool her. Even in this relaxed stance every fiber of his being seemed to be standing at attention. What had him on edge? Maybe he was suffering from PTSD.

She'd been plagued by the same ailment, and a lot more, after Alex's murder. If she opened up to J.D. about it, maybe he'd open up to her.

She snorted and aimed her beam of light onto the dirt path to the guesthouse. J.D. was here to work, not get psychoanalyzed.

"Wait up." He scuffled behind her. "You're the one with the light."

She slowed down just enough so that he could catch up to the light but not enough for him to be breathing down her back. He'd probably laugh in her face if he could hear all her ridiculous thoughts about him.

He still had the keys, so when they reached the guesthouse she stopped and illuminated the doorknob.

"No dead bolt here either?" He shoved the key in the lock and turned. He pushed the door open with the toe of his boot.

A musty smell engulfed Noelle as J.D. waved her through the door ahead of him.

"I could've cleaned up first if you'd waited a day." She flicked on a light switch, which turned on a lamp.

"Are there clean sheets on the bed?"

Why did he have to keep saying that word? She snapped her fingers. "No, but I'll bring them from the house."

She left him to inspect the rest of the house, and retraced their steps. The flashlight sweeping in front of her, she scurried to the house and grabbed a set of sheets from the linen closet in the hallway. Clutching the sheets to her chest with one arm, she rushed to the guesthouse. She hoped J.D. could make a bed by himself, because she couldn't face him across a mattress.

She walked into the house, burying her nose in the freshly laundered scent of the sheets to blot out the mustiness of the house. She dropped the pile of linens on the couch, and J.D. turned from inspecting the window.

"Do you think someone's going to break in here, too?"

He tapped a finger on the glass. "Anything's possible. If there are…junkies looking for a quick fix they might hit this place, too. Especially once it looks inhabited."

Noelle assessed J.D.'s strong physique. This time the thieves might get a surprise. Could it really be just a couple of low-level junkies like Sheriff Greavy and her missing meds suggested? Maybe this break-in had nothing to do with the break-in at her place in D.C. Just another ding in her long spiral of bad luck since Alex's death. She shivered.

"Are you okay?" J.D. dug his cell phone from his front pocket. "Give me your number. I'll call you and you can add my cell number to your contacts. If anything else happens tonight, give me a call. I don't think they'll be back. They got what they came for."

Did they?

She gave him her number, he called her phone and she stored it under his name. That made their connection seem more real. Of course, having him around the ranch every day would seem pretty real, too.

"I'll walk you back if you let me take the flashlight. One of my first chores will be to get some floodlights set up on the outside of the ranch."

"Okay." She bit her lip and surveyed the room. "You can get to work on this place first if you want."

"Don't worry about me. This is fine." He took her arm and pulled her through the front door. "It's late. We can work out the rest of the details later."

Details? They had details to work out? Must be talking about the money.

Once outside on the path back to the ranch house, Noelle shook off J.D.'s light grasp from her arm. She'd been so wary of strangers the past few years and yet she'd invited this man onto her ranch and into her life in less than twenty-four hours of acquaintance. She'd have to fire up her laptop and do a thorough search on Jim Davis. How many millions would she have to sift through to find this one?

J.D. lifted the screen door and held it up while she unlocked the door.

"Here you go." She handed him the flashlight. "We'll discuss the rest of the…uh…details tomorrow. You can drop by for breakfast."

"I'd like that."

"Good night, then." She slipped into the house before she could do something foolish. It was too soon after Alex's death to get romantically involved with someone.

Two years. Was that too soon? Given the circumstances, ten years would be too soon.

She waited a few minutes, her palms flat against the front door. Then she slipped outside and picked her way across the dirt driveway to her truck. She unlocked the passenger door and reached beneath the seat to retrieve her laptop.

Hugging the computer to her chest, she returned to the house and locked the door behind her. Maybe J.D.'s first order of business should be a dead bolt for that front door.

Odd that a petty thief or junkie knew how to pick a lock without leaving a trace.

But then, the people who had broken into her place in D.C. hadn't been too concerned about leaving behind a trail of destruction and upheaval. Maybe she just had a streak of bad luck following her—or picking up on her trail again.

She sighed and plunked the laptop onto the kitchen counter. She powered it on and poured a glass of water.

"Jim Davis." She said the name as she typed it onto the screen. Realtors, actors, musicians and criminals popped up. She took a sip of water and swished it around in her mouth.

"Jim Davis, Texas." Hadn't J.D. mentioned he hailed from Texas? Adding the state narrowed the search but not by much. She tried James Davis without any more luck.

She powered down the laptop and snapped it shut. Too bad her newly acquired ranch hand didn't have a more unusual name. She dumped the water into the sink and turned off the light in the kitchen.

If she didn't trust J.D., she could always ask him to leave. But he'd helped her out of a jam—twice. She didn't care if the stranger had something to hide as long as it didn't impact her.

She flicked off a few more lights on her way to the bedroom, and then she hit the bathroom to wash her face and brush her teeth. She'd wanted that guesthouse as a studio, but maybe J.D. could fix the basics in there before she removed the furniture and installed a skylight.

She turned down the bed and placed her slippers side by side at the foot of the bed. She straightened the alarm clock, lining up the edge along the grain of wood.

She caught her breath. Closing her eyes, she folded her hands and exhaled through her nostrils. It was the stress. She didn't need medication. She'd force herself to relax.

She climbed into bed, sliding between the fresh sheets. She reached for the lamp on the nightstand, and her gaze snagged on the picture on the wall across the room. The right corner tilted higher than the left.

Leave it.

She punched the light switch on the base of the lamp. Her eyes grew accustomed to the gloom, and she picked out the edge of the picture in the darkness. She squeezed her lids shut.

"Okay, this is it. The last time." She turned the light back on and threw back her covers.

She stalked toward the picture, gritting her teeth. She grabbed the frame with both hands and inched up the left side. As she slid her fingers off the glass, the pad of her thumb stumbled over a dab of something on the frame.

She ran her fingers across the area again and felt the nodule on the glass. Drawing her brows over her nose, she leaned in for a closer look.

A tiny eye stared back at her.

Chapter Six

J.D. pulled the clean sheets up to his chest and inhaled the smell of grass and sunshine on a cold winter night. It smelled as if the linen had been hung out to dry in the spring and the scent had clung to the folds of the cotton through the dead of winter. How had Noelle done that? Or was he just imagining the smell?

He rolled to his side, anticipating sleep to steal over his limbs, heavy with exhaustion. Instead, a bang on the front door had him bolting upright in the bed, all thoughts of spring evaporating.

At the second bang, he kicked off the covers and stumbled to the front door. A quick glance out the window revealed Noelle parked on the porch, her fists raised for another assault.

He yanked open the door, and she almost fell into his arms. And he would've welcomed it.

One look at her wide eyes in her pale face and his heart slammed against his chest. "What's wrong?"

She held out her thumb and index finger pinched together, trembling. "I—I found something in my bedroom."

Was she afraid of a little bug? He extended his palm. "What is it?"

She released her fingers, dropping a black button into

his hand. He brought it close to his face. Then he crushed it in his fist.

A camera.

"It's some kind of camera, isn't it?" She crossed her arms over her chest.

Now he knew it hadn't been druggies who had broken into her house. The spy camera bit into his flesh. "Where did you find this? How?"

"It was stuck on a picture frame in my bedroom." She hunched her shoulders, tightening the grip on her arms. "I felt it first."

He didn't ask why she'd been feeling a picture frame in the middle of the night. He dropped the disabled device on the table. "Why would someone be spying on you?"

"I have no idea."

He did.

Should he tell her now? Would she be in greater danger knowing about the threat against her? If he told her, would she run? He'd gotten orders from Prospero to keep Noelle in the dark until they could assess how much she knew, but why was she keeping *him* in the dark?

He'd been waiting for her to tell him about the D.C. break-in ever since someone had pulled the same trick at the ranch. She hadn't said a word to him about it.

Clasping her shoulders through the thick terry cloth of her bathrobe, he said, "Is someone after you? Bad divorce? Dumped boyfriend?"

She wriggled out of his grasp. "Of course not."

"Was anyone following you back in D.C.?"

Come on, Noelle. Tell me about your missing roommate. Tell me about your ransacked apartment. Trust me.

Her deep blue eyes flickered, but she shook her head. "No."

"Any enemies here?"

"Not that I know of."

"Your half brother?"

"Why would he spy on me?"

"He wants the ranch. He wants to keep an eye on you."

She shivered and yanked on the sash of her robe. "I—I don't think so."

"You've shot down every suggestion I made." He crossed his arms over his bare chest, the chill of the night causing goose bumps to march across his flesh. "What do you think? Why did you run over here if not for my advice?"

"I'm not sure. Finding that thing scared the heck out of me." Her cheeks flamed.

She'd come to the guesthouse ready to spill everything, but something had stopped her. He rubbed his arms. She didn't trust him…yet. "I'm sorry."

"Sorry?"

"You came here looking for some comfort, and I'm giving you the third degree." He yanked on the ties of her robe, pulling her into his realm.

Her body stiffened, so he stopped short of dragging her into his arms. He brushed the back of his hand along her smooth cheek. "What do you want me to do?"

"If you could just—" her gaze finally dropped from his eyes to his chest, continuing down to the unbuttoned fly of the jeans he'd hastily pulled on when she'd pounded on his door "—come back to the house."

His skin heated beneath her bold inventory. Despite the electric current between them, this was the first time she'd looked at him like a woman looked at a man. He liked it.

He shoved his personal attraction to her into a little corner of his brain. She must be scared if she trusted him enough to invite him to spend the night in her house, and he had to honor that trust.

He cupped her face with one hand. "I'd be happy to

bunk on the couch. I'm not sure the furnace is working in this place, anyway."

He also knew if Zendaris's men had placed a hidden camera in her bedroom, they'd probably outfitted the other rooms as well, and he had just the device to detect any other cameras. He held up one finger. "Hang on while I gather a few things."

She nodded and wedged a shoulder against the door-jamb.

J.D. grabbed the black backpack he'd retrieved from his truck before he'd turned in and shoved several items inside, making sure to include his weapon.

Noelle had brought another flashlight with her. Now two beams of light bobbed across the dirt and gravel back to the main house.

If she'd just open up to him about the disappearance of Abby Warren and the break-in at her D.C. place, he could confirm to Prospero that she didn't know a thing about Zendaris or Abby's involvement in his plans. Maybe a few more weeks with him playing the helpful cowboy would loosen her tongue.

They got back to the house and she locked the front door. "I was thinking your first order of business could be a dead bolt on this door."

"I was thinking the same thing, along with those motion-sensor lights I mentioned earlier. You need to tell the sheriff about this recent development. He needs to look beyond the local junkies. Someone's stalking you."

"I can't imagine why, unless…" She wrapped her po-nytail around her hand.

"Unless what?" He held his breath.

"Maybe you'd better sit down for this."

You show me yours, Noelle, and I'll show you mine.

He followed her to the couch and sat on the opposite end—time enough to move closer.

She clasped her hands between her knees. "I'm a widow."

"I'm sorry."

"My husband was murdered two years ago at the art gallery where he worked."

"Burglars?"

"Yes." She closed her eyes, and a spasm of pain crossed her face.

She must've loved him. No wonder she couldn't warm up to another man.

"That's terrible, Noelle, but what does that have to do with your present situation?"

Her eyes flew open and she pinned him with a blue-violet gaze. "I was there. I witnessed his murder, and his killers got away. The police never did catch them."

He knew all of it, but he raised his eyebrows and dropped his jaw. "That must've been traumatic for you."

"It was, but don't you see?" She hunched forward. "Maybe the men who killed my husband are after me now."

He eased back against the sofa cushion. If this was what she thought, she'd had no inclination of what her room-mate was up to.

"Why would they be after you? Did you ID them?"

"They were wearing masks. I could never give the police a description. To me they seemed ten feet tall, monsters wielding guns."

Leaning forward, he covered her bunched hands with one of his. "Why would they be after you now if you never identified them? It's been two years, Noelle. If you haven't given the police a description by now, you never will. They know that."

"I don't know whether I want it to be them or not." She

collapsed against the back of the couch. "I can't think of who else it could be."

"Don't worry about it right now." He squeezed her hands, still cold even covered by his. "Get some sleep. We'll take the camera to Sheriff Greavy tomorrow and let him figure it out. In the meantime, I'll be here keeping watch."

She slipped her hands from beneath his and stood up. "I hope you'll get some sleep, too. I still plan to work you hard."

That thought sent a pleasant buzz to his…fingertips. "Yes, ma'am."

"I'll get you a pillow and a couple of blankets for the couch."

"Do you happen to have a toothbrush I can use?"

"Of course." She retreated to the hallway with a flip of her silky ponytail.

J.D. pulled off his boots and stashed his backpack on the floor between the couch and the coffee table.

Noelle returned and dumped the blankets and pillow on the couch and placed an unwrapped toothbrush on the coffee table.

"Thanks."

"Thank *you*. You've been a big help today, like a guardian angel."

He snorted as he could feel his ears burning. "Not quite."

They said good-night and she pulled her door shut as he headed into the bathroom to brush his teeth. Several seconds later, the lock on the bedroom door clicked into place.

Guess there were limits to how far she could trust a guardian angel.

J.D. rinsed his mouth, tapped his wet toothbrush on the edge of the sink and left it on the vanity. He crept past Noelle's locked door on his way back to the living room and unzipped his backpack. He placed his weapon beneath a cushion on the couch and dug for his radio-frequency detector.

With a sweeping motion, he scanned the living room, cocking his head to listen for a hit. If Zendaris and his thugs were monitoring the feed from the camera or multiple cameras, they'd see him looking for the device.

They'd know Noelle had company. They'd know she had protection. They'd know she had someone on her side. So what?

Let the games begin.

NOELLE STARED AT the picture where she'd found the camera. She'd sort of assumed the D.C. break-in might have been related to Alex's murder and had been hoping the one at the ranch was just what the sheriff thought it was—junkies looking for a quick fix. The discovery of that hidden camera had torpedoed that theory.

J.D. made sense. Why would Alex's killers be after her now, two years later, when she hadn't been able to give the police one clue to their identities?

She had no enemies. No ex-boyfriends. No secret stalkers—even Bruce didn't fall into that category. The murder of her husband had been the only less-than-ordinary event in her life. It had overshadowed everything else before and since.

"Abby." She whispered the name of her former roommate.

Could this have something to do with Abby? Was someone looking for her roommate? Abby's family hadn't even called her to ask questions. She knew Abby had a sister, at least. Was this their way of finding out what had happened to Abby?

She closed her eyes and dug her fists beneath her pillow. She'd report this new affront to Sheriff Greavy tomorrow, have J.D. replace every lock in the place and sleep with a loaded shotgun next to her bed every night.

She'd been jumping at shadows for the past two years. Now that she had something to jump at, it was time to dig in and put up a fight.

She froze. Someone was tapping on the walls. Someone? J.D. was tapping on the walls.

Had she been insane allowing a stranger into her home? She knew nothing about Jim Davis. *Jim Davis.* What a conveniently common name.

He could be the one stalking her. Maybe he had broken into the house after running into her in the parking lot of the grocery store. Maybe he had disabled her car. Maybe he had planted the camera.

Her mind had been working this way ever since Alex's murder. Suspicions. Doubts. Mistrust. It had been her armor. It had steered her away from any possible relationship— well, that and her guilt.

Why had her defenses failed her now? She'd been approached by good-looking guys before, so it wasn't J.D.'s tawny hair and matching eyes or his solid muscles or the way his grin spread across his face, slow and easy.

As attractive as she found the man, his appearance had been secondary in her assessment. It had been all about the way he'd taken care of her, protected her, looked out for her. When had she ever had someone like that in her life?

She'd been the one to take care of Alex in their marriage...and she'd failed at it.

The tapping continued, and she rolled out of bed. J.D. made her feel safe, but it could all be an act. Bottom line— she had a strange man in her house and he seemed to be searching for something in the middle of the night.

She grabbed the shotgun from the corner. Then she crept across the floor and unlocked her door, turning the handle a centimeter at a time. She nudged the door open with her hip and slipped into the hallway.

Pressing the gun against her side, she narrowed her eyes as she peered across the darkened living room at J.D. He hadn't heard her yet and continued creeping around the edges of the room, one hand held in front of him.

She swallowed and raised her shotgun.

"Who the hell are you, and what are you doing in my house?"

Chapter Seven

J.D. spun around, dipped his right hand into his pocket and thrust his hands above his head. That stance came a little too naturally to him.

Noelle tightened her grip on the shotgun. "What are you looking for? What do you want from me?"

His gesture turned to one of supplication as he held his hands out, palms up. "Take it easy. It occurred to me when I was lying there trying to get to sleep that if your stalker planted one spy camera, he might've planted others. I was just checking out the room."

She licked her lips. "H-how were you looking? What were you looking for? I just happened to find the camera because the picture frame was crooked."

"Looking at the same types of places—picture frames, the mirror, plants." He shrugged. "I've seen a few spy movies in my day."

Was he feeding her a line? Conning her? Ted had been the master of cons, and she'd learned to spot one a mile away. She didn't get the sense that J.D. meant her any harm.

She blew out a shaky breath. "What did you have in your hand when I walked in?"

He dropped his arms and fished in the front pocket of

his jeans. "My cell phone. I heard you could actually pick up frequencies with your cell phone."

"You weren't kidding about those spy movies, were you?" She leaned the shotgun against the wall. "I'm sorry I pointed a gun at you."

"I understand. In fact, if it hadn't been me that you were inviting into your home, I would've chastised you for allowing a relative stranger to spend the night under the same roof with you."

"I surprised myself, but the camera scared me and you had already rescued me a few times today." She tilted her head, searching for more words to explain the affinity she felt for him, the way he eased through the chinks of her armor.

She tossed her ponytail over one shoulder. Maybe Dr. Eliason had done enough head shrinking on her so that she could finally let down her defenses. Perfect timing— just when someone was stalking her for real. Maybe it had taken a real threat to break through her shell.

Maybe it had taken J.D.

"I don't want you to be worried, Noelle. I'll secure these locks tomorrow. You keep that shotgun close and you'll be fine in this house by yourself. I'll make myself comfortable in the guesthouse."

She hoisted the gun. "Do you want me to help you look for more devices?"

"Are you going to shoot at them?"

"Not a bad idea."

"It's way past midnight. You get some sleep—" he held up his cell phone "—and I'll continue the search."

Sounded like a dismissal to her. Maybe she'd scared him off with the shotgun and her whiplash-inducing change of moods. She tucked the gun against her side and trooped down the hallway, calling over her shoulder, "Good luck."

THE FOLLOWING MORNING, the rich scent of coffee tickled her nostrils. She opened one eye, and her gaze trailed to the picture across the room. Ironic that the stalker had hidden the camera on the frame of one of Alex's pictures—as if Alex himself was keeping an eye on her from the grave.

What would Alex think about the man in the other room?

She kicked her feet over the side of the bed and tucked them into her slippers. The sounds from the kitchen drew her down the hall, and she peeked around the corner.

J.D. raised a spatula in greeting. "I'm not the best cook in the world, but I can handle something simple."

"The coffee smells great." She sat on a stool at the kitchen island, the tips of her slippers scuffing the tile floor.

He held up the pot from the coffeemaker. "Hard to screw up coffee."

"But not toast." She leveled a finger at the smoking toaster oven.

"Those are bagels." He yanked down the door of the toaster oven and forked a bagel half onto a plate. "The edges are a little crispy, but I think it's still good."

She took the plate from him and scooped a knife into the tub of butter he'd placed in front of her. The butter melted on the warm bagel, running over the sides and puddling on the plate. She licked her fingers.

"Did you have any luck finding more cameras?" She glanced over her shoulder. "They could be watching us right now."

"I think the one in your bedroom was the only one." He splashed some milk in his mug of coffee and held up the carton.

She shoved her cup of coffee toward him and he poured a steady stream of milk into the brown liquid. She held up her hand when the milk had turned the coffee into a toffee color—not quite the shade of J.D.'s eyes.

"I'm going into town to talk to Sheriff Greavy today. I'd like to show him the camera I found last night."

"Good idea. I'm going in, too, to pick up some supplies."

"I'll take you."

He bit into his bagel and chewed, and she had to restrain herself from dabbing at the buttery crumb at the corner of his mouth.

"Let's take my truck. Your vehicle has seen better days."

"That was my dad's truck. A neighbor, one of my dad's friends, had been keeping it for me. I don't even have a car in D.C."

"What do you do in D.C.?"

"I'm a curator at an art museum."

J.D. jerked up his head and twisted it from side to side, scanning the room. "Did you paint all of these?"

"Some of them."

He half closed his eyes and tilted back his head. "There are two different styles—one cheerful and optimistic and the other darker, more introspective."

She raised her hand. "I'm the dark, introspective one."

"And the cheerful one?"

"My husband."

"He was an artist, too?"

"A much better one." Her words tumbled over each other. "He was the real talent in the family."

"It's in the eye of the beholder, I guess." He nibbled on the side of his thumb. "I guess I find the moody stuff more interesting."

Warmth crept into her cheeks and she dipped her head to sip her coffee. Yet another betrayal of Alex. Her art had been getting more attention than his toward the end. After he died, she'd given it up. To continue with her art

when he was dead and gone seemed even more traitorous than the feelings she'd had toward him at the time
of his death.

"Sorry. Didn't mean to bring up painful memories." He
brushed his hands together over the sink. "You did say the
shower in the guesthouse worked, didn't you?"

"Uh-huh."

"Then I'll head back over there and get cleaned up before I take you into town. I need to stop by my hotel and
pick up my bag and check out."

She laced her fingers around her coffee cup. How had
she allowed this man to take such complete control over
her life in such a short space of time? She had to gain the
upper hand. He worked for her, and yet he knew more
about her life than she did about his. "J.D.?"

"Yeah?" He cranked on the faucet and held his plate
under the stream of water.

"What brought you to Buck Ridge after you were discharged from the service? And what branch of the service
were you in?" Holding her breath, she studied his reaction, but her questions didn't seem to disturb him at all.

"Semper fi." He flashed a grin. "I came out to Buck
Ridge for the skiing. Thought maybe I could pick up work
as an instructor, but I got here too late. I liked the look of
the place and decided to stick around."

She dug in her heels. "Where's your family?"

"My parents are at their ranch in Texas. I have a couple
of sisters who are busy getting on with their own lives."
He rinsed his cup and put the dishes in the dish drainer on
the counter. "I'm wandering right now, Noelle. I want the
freedom to pack up and leave whenever I want. Do you
have a problem with that?"

"Me?" She ran her hands across her face, smoothing

out the lines. "Not at all. Just give me a little notice before you pack up and leave."

"Will do."

She hopped off the stool to extinguish the disappointment that flared in her gut. Why should it surprise her that J.D. had plans to move on? "I'm gonna hit that shower now." He tossed a dish towel onto the counter, snagged his backpack and strolled toward the front door.

She followed him and watched him cross the yard to the guesthouse, his long, confident stride eating up the ground beneath him. She didn't expect him to settle in the guesthouse forever, but if he wanted to stay there until she felt safe, she wouldn't mind that one bit.

J.D. FLICKED THE disabled spy camera he'd uncovered last night into an ashtray next to the one Noelle had found.

While Noelle had slept, he'd searched the rest of the house, but Zendaris seemed to have been satisfied outfitting just Noelle's bedroom and her living room. What the hell did Zendaris think Noelle knew about Abby and where she'd hidden the plans for the anti-drone?

What did Prospero think she knew?

They were both wrong. She didn't know anything. She still believed this harassment had something to do with her husband's murder, not even connecting it to the disappearance of her roommate.

What had the D.C. cops told Noelle about Abby, anyway? He knew they hadn't made a big deal out of it. Maybe that's why Noelle hadn't mentioned it to him yet. But then, she kept things zipped up.

After opening up about her husband, she'd stacked up her defenses again. She ran hot and cold. When she got the sense she'd told him too much, she'd shut down. Then she'd turned the questioning on him.

He didn't mind. He had his story down—half-truths made it sound more believable. His sisters were getting on with their lives all right, but they were dragging him along with them by sending him pictures of their kids every two minutes. His parents were on the ranch, but they were joining his sisters every five minutes, begging him to come back to the ranch for a visit.

He couldn't allow Noelle to see his phone or she'd wonder what the hell he was doing hanging out in a town where he didn't know anyone except her when his family back in Texas was begging him to check in for a visit. Ever since his fiancée had dumped him, his sisters had been busy trying to set him up.

He didn't need setting up. He could find his own woman.

Thirty minutes later, wearing the same clothes as yesterday, he clapped his hat on his head and sauntered into the yard. He spotted Noelle sitting on the porch railing, swinging one booted foot.

He cupped one hand around his mouth and yelled, "Be careful. That thing might collapse beneath you."

She scooted off and landed on the dirt, pulling an oversize bag with her. "I think I found the one stable spot." She tapped her head. "The hat looks new."

J.D. ran his hands along the brim. He hadn't had time to head home and pack clothes more appropriate for a ranch than the big city, so he'd picked up a few things to look the part. "Didn't have much use for a cowboy hat in Iraq."

"I wouldn't think so. Did the shower and—" she waved her hand up and down his body "—everything else work okay?"

"Warm water and everything."

"Where's your truck? I didn't even notice last night that it wasn't inside the gates."

"When I saw your brother heading onto your land last night, I pulled my truck over outside your gates so I could take him by surprise."

"Well, you did that."

He chuckled at the memory. He'd wondered why he was able to take down one of Zendaris's guys so easily. "I did not break his nose."

"Ted tends to get overly dramatic. He's a great actor." Her shoulder jostled against his as they walked out to his truck, and she took a step away from him.

"What's his story?" He beeped his remote to unlock his truck, then got the door for Noelle. She climbed into the truck without answering.

He repeated the question when he slid into the driver's seat.

"He's a user, in more ways than one." She shrugged. "I guess he's clean and sober again. Maybe it'll stick this time."

"Did he depend on you a lot?"

Before pulling onto the road, J.D. checked his rear-view mirror.

"Anyone following us?"

"I thought I was being discreet."

"Why bother? It's not like I don't know I have a target on my back...for some reason."

Noelle didn't know the ones who had put that target on her back were expert marksmen. Should he scrap protocol and tell her?

"Maybe it's not a bad idea to have your brother move in with you." As unreliable as Ted Dupree seemed, it might work in Noelle's favor to be surrounded by people.

"I've always helped out Ted. My ther...people have been

telling me to stop enabling him. I want to see if he can stand on his own and stay sober before I open my life up to him again."

"That's probably good advice." He tapped the inside of the windshield. "Looks like we're getting a dusting of snow."

"The skiers will be happy."

"Do you ski?"

"Yeah, but I'm no expert. Spent a lot of my time here doing other activities. You must be good if you considered being an instructor."

"I've done my share of skiing, but I've started snowboarding more lately. Does the Buck Ridge Resort allow snowboarders, too?"

"They had to if they wanted to attract a younger crowd." She jerked her thumb to the side. "You can turn here to get into town. Are you going to talk to Sheriff Greavy with me or just drop me off?"

"I'll come in with you. Do you have something to do while I pick up supplies, or do you want to come along?"

"I'll leave the supplies to you. I have plenty to do." She reached into her bag and held out a credit card pinched between her fingers. "Just don't forget the lock."

"What's that for?"

"All the supplies. You're just doing the work. You don't have to finance it."

"Maybe you'd better come along, then. I don't want to go over budget."

Noelle had a substantial sum of money in the bank. Prospero had already checked it out to make sure she hadn't acquired it recently. She hadn't. The money had been sitting in that account for a few years, and she hadn't spent a dime of it.

"I haven't done anything to that ranch since my parents

left it to me, so it's due for a face-lift. Spend what you need and give me the receipts."

"Yes, ma'am."

She directed him to the sheriff's station, and he pulled his car into the side parking lot.

J.D. put his hat on, protecting his head from the silvery snow flurries, and Noelle pulled her hood up; the white fur framed her face.

He shoved the door open for her and ushered her in first.

She greeted the sergeant at the desk. "Hey, Chris, is Sheriff Greavy in?"

"He's on a call. It's been a busy morning. Lots of skiers scrambling to get to the resort."

"This is J.D. He's going to be helping out at the ranch. J.D., this is Sergeant Chris Malone."

J.D. pulled off his glove and shook hands with the sergeant, who gave him the once-over.

"Do you know about the break-in at my place last night?"

"I heard about it. I'll be glad when the ski season's over and we can get back to some peace and quiet around here. Crime seems to come with the tourists." He shot a look at J.D. that seemed to include him with the criminals or the tourists.

Noelle smacked the little camera on the counter. "I think this is more than a simple crime."

Sergeant Malone bent forward to inspect the black button. "Is that a minicamera?"

"Yep. On a picture frame. In my bedroom."

The sergeant whistled. "Sounds like you got yourself a perv, Noelle." He flashed another glance at J.D.

J.D. gritted his teeth and nodded. "You have any other reports of similar infractions, Sergeant?"

"Infractions?"

Damn. I'll have to stop talking like law enforcement.

"Any other women reporting Peeping Toms or anything like that?"

"Not down here. A few incidents up at the ski lodge. Doesn't mean the pervs didn't make their way off the mountain."

"That's comforting."

J.D. hunched over the counter and tried to sound like an amateur. "Do you think you can trace it? Get fingerprints?"

Pinching the camera between his thumb and index fingers, Sergeant Malone brought it close to his face and squinted at it. "No fingerprints for sure. If you had called us when you found it, Noelle, we might've had a chance."

No, you wouldn't have.

She lifted a shoulder. "I wasn't going to leave that thing in my room. Can you trace the model or something, like J.D. said?"

"You can buy these online." Malone bounced it in the palm of his hand. "There's no way we can trace this."

"I'll leave it with you. Let me know if you hear of anything else like this."

The sergeant blew into a small plastic bag to puff it open. "I heard Teddy's in town."

"You, too?" She wedged her hands on her hips. "I might believe he'd steal some prescription meds, although he swears he's clean, but sticking cameras in my bedroom? Not his style."

"You always were one to defend that boy. I'm not saying he's a Peeping Tom, but he might want to keep an eye on your comings and goings, your—" Sergeant Malone cleared his throat and flicked a glance at J.D. "—associations."

"I don't think Ted cared one way or the other that I got the ranch. It didn't mean anything to him."

Malone scratched his chin. "Maybe not when he was high as a kite but if he's really clean, he might be more interested in the ranch now."

"Ted expected to crash at the ranch. He wouldn't have needed a camera."

"And you turned him away?" Malone winked. "It's about time."

Noelle bit her lip, obviously not comfortable with the sergeant's praise. "Tell Sheriff Greavy about this latest development, and let me know if you come up with anything."

"Will do." He waved the plastic evidence bag containing the camera.

As they emerged onto the sidewalk, J.D. squeezed Noelle's shoulder. "Are you okay? The sergeant didn't change your mind about Ted, did he? You were right. If he thought he was going to stay at the ranch, he had no need to plant a camera."

"I'm still sure Ted had nothing to do with the break-in. I'm just wondering if I did the right thing by turning him away."

He took her other shoulder and turned her to face him. "You have the right instincts. Let him prove himself before you make any commitments to him or he'll suck you in again."

Her lips began to curve into a smile.

"Noelle! Noelle!"

Her gaze skittered past his shoulder and the smile froze. Her body stiffened. She gasped.

"What's wrong?" J.D. glanced behind him and picked

out a man in a brightly colored jacket and a hat with earflaps jogging toward them.

"That just might be my stalker."

Chapter Eight

J.D. squeezed her shoulders once more before spinning around to face Bruce with her.

Bruce reached them, his face flushed, snow droplets clinging to his ridiculous furry earflaps. A most unlikely stalker...but Noelle knew better.

He pulled her into an awkward, one-armed hug. Awkward because Noelle kept her frame stiff and unyielding. How many hints did she have to give this guy? And what was he doing in Colorado?

When Bruce reached for her, Noelle could feel J.D. tense beside her. She'd better explain things before J.D. started whaling on Bruce, just as he had on Ted.

Not a bad idea.

She broke away from Bruce's embrace. "What are you doing here?"

"When the museum said you were on an extended vacation, I knew you'd come back here. Where else? You and Alex were happy here." He tugged at his earflaps. "Is this your brother?"

His words rose in a hopeful tone.

"No. This is J.D. He's helping me out at the ranch. J.D., this is Bruce Pierpont."

"Friend from D.C.?" J.D. shook Bruce's hand long and hard—really hard.

When the clasp ended, Bruce shoved his gloved hand in his pocket as if to hide it from J.D. in case he decided to grab it again.

"Noelle and I are old friends. My family collects art, and we really saw something in Noelle…. Alex, too. You could say we're patrons of the arts."

"Did she invite you out here?" J.D. crossed his arms, looking even bigger and more menacing in his black duster.

Taking a step back, Bruce waved his hand in the air. "Not precisely, but she and her husband gifted me with a standing invitation and I was due for a ski trip. I had offered to turn the guesthouse on the ranch into an art studio for the two of them. Have you seen that guesthouse? The light is divine."

"I'm living there, and you're right. The light *is* divine."

Noelle covered her mouth with her hand and coughed.

Bruce turned a shoulder to J.D. and took Noelle's hands. "Let's have dinner tonight. I'm staying up at the lodge and, from all accounts, the best restaurant in Buck Ridge is right in the hotel. I'm familiar with the head chef's cuisine."

J.D. slapped Bruce on the back. "I've been wanting to try that place. Thanks for the invite."

"Seven o'clock good for you, Bruce?" Noelle pinned a sweet smile on her face.

Stammering, Bruce's face reddened as his gaze flicked to J.D. Then years of good breeding won the day and he matched her smile.

"Seven o'clock would be perfect. I'm going to try to get in a little afternoon skiing." He raised his eyes skyward, holding out one hand to catch the snow flurries.

"We'll meet you there. Enjoy your skiing." Noelle sidled up against J.D.'s shoulder just in case Bruce decided to grab her for another hug.

Instead he leaned forward and planted a kiss on her

cheek with a pair of cold, dry lips. "See you tonight. We can discuss plans for that studio."

They both watched Bruce clump down the sidewalk in obviously new snow boots, and then J.D. snorted.

"You think that's your stalker?"

"Let's get out of this snow, and I'll tell you about Bruce Pierpont." She tipped her chin toward a coffeehouse on the corner. "In there."

Noelle snagged a table in the corner by the fireplace while J.D. ordered their drinks.

"I got the works on your hot chocolate—whipped cream and chocolate shavings." He put the concoction on the table and sat across from her, cradling a mug of steaming black coffee.

She licked a fluff of whipped cream from the towering mound floating on the top of her hot chocolate. Closing her eyes, she savored the sweet creaminess that melted on her tongue.

"Good, huh?"

Her eyelids flew open, and she met J.D.'s amber gaze. His eyes kindled, and she felt the heat right down to the tips of her toes. He probably thought she'd been trying to come on to him with the whole whipped-cream act.

When she came on to him, he'd know it.

Not that she had any intention of doing so. She slurped her chocolate through the cream and burned her tongue. "It's delicious."

He raised one eyebrow. "Tell me about Bruce Pierpont."

"He's loaded, in case you couldn't figure that out. Comes from a wealthy family, silver spoon firmly clenched between his teeth."

"I know someone like that, but you'd never guess he comes from money—not like Pierpont, who oozes that upper-crust vibe." He swirled his coffee. "How'd you meet him?"

"He came to one of Alex's exhibits. It's true what he said. His family supports the arts and part of that is backing new, young artists."

"Did he switch his allegiance from Alex to you?"

"Not right away. That came gradually."

"Along with his gradual attraction to you?"

She set down her mug too quickly, and the brown liquid sloshed over the sides. "Yes."

"And Alex figured it all out."

"He accused…" She pressed her lips together. She wouldn't say anything bad about Alex. He wasn't here to give his side of the story. "We both figured it out and stepped away from Bruce for a while."

"Did Bruce step back in when Alex died?"

"Yeah, all solicitous and helpful."

"And stalkerish."

"Not really."

J.D. choked on his coffee and grabbed a napkin to wipe his eyes. "Excuse me? When you saw him on the street, you said you'd found your stalker."

"I said he *might* be my stalker." She planted her elbows on the table and cupped her chin with one hand. "Don't you think it's suspicious that he showed up here the day after someone breaks into my house and hides a camera in my bedroom?"

"Your brother showed up about the same time. What makes you suspect Bruce more?"

With her elbows still on the table, she covered her face with her splayed hands. "I haven't told you everything."

Silence greeted her from across the table, and she peeked at J.D. through her fingers.

He shrugged and took a sip of his coffee. "You're not obligated to tell me anything— unless you want to."

Folding her hands on the table, she took a deep breath. "Someone broke into my place in D.C., too. That's part of the reason why I wanted to escape the city."

"Same thing in D.C.? Someone slipped in and stole some meds?" He crushed the napkin in his hand.

"Completely different. Someone ransacked my place, and I didn't find anything missing."

"What about a hidden camera there? Could someone have bugged your place?"

A sick dread twisted her insides. She hadn't wanted to think about that before, but it made sense. "Maybe that's how they knew I was headed to Buck Ridge."

"Is Bruce Pierpont off the hook now? He wouldn't have had to bug your apartment to know you had a house here."

"I don't know." She buried her fingers in her hair. "Maybe there was no hidden camera at my place in D.C. Now that I know your cell-phone trick, I should go back there and search for it."

"If it is Bruce keeping tabs on you, at least you know why. If it's not Bruce, what possible reason would someone have to search your place and then tag along after you to Buck Ridge?"

"Search?"

"What?"

"You said *search*. Do you think someone's searching for something?"

J.D. flattened the napkin on the table and ran his thumb along the creases. "If the same person—or people—broke into both places, it stands to reason. They trashed your apartment in D.C. without taking anything. This time they were more careful—probably didn't want you to know you'd been followed."

"Sounds like you've really given this some thought. Go on."

"It's just common sense. Out here, they didn't want to be obvious, but just in case you did notice someone had been in your house they stole some prescription meds out of the bathroom so the break-in could be brushed off as a petty theft."

"Wow, you're good." *Too good.* Leaning back in her chair, she crossed her arms across her stomach. "Almost like you have the mind of a criminal yourself."

"You're not going to point a shotgun at me again, are you?"

She formed her fingers into a pistol and shot it at him. "You have the how figured out. Now give me the who and the why and I'll declare you a genius."

He dragged a finger through her rapidly melting whipped cream and aimed it at her. "You tell me the why. Do you have something that someone wants?"

"I was going to finish that." She eyed his index finger dripping cream onto the table.

"You're avoiding the question."

"I'm not avoiding it. I don't have anything that anyone would want. All my money's locked up in a bank. All my artwork is in storage—and I *wish* someone wanted my paintings that badly."

"Did anyone give you anything for safekeeping?"

"No."

J.D. slouched back in his chair, the tension melting from his frame as fast as that whipped cream had melted into her chocolate.

"You're completely in the dark."

"That doesn't sound like a question, but I'm going to answer it anyway. Yes. I'm completely in the dark. I had one traumatic event in my life. One reason why someone might be after me. And as you pointed out before, there would be no reason for Alex's killers to harass me now."

"That one event was enough, but it doesn't have to be a trauma. It could be something out of the ordinary, something you didn't give much thought to at the time." He steepled his fingers and peered at her over the tips. "Nothing like that?"

The fact that her roommate had disappeared without giving any notice ranked up there as something out of the ordinary, but maybe just to her. The cops hadn't seemed to attach much significance to it at the time. Other people got up and moved, took risks, had adventures. Look at J.D. Discharged from the service and traveling the country.

She'd been so risk-averse since Alex's murder, she couldn't even switch shampoos. She shook her head. "Nothing."

J.D.'s eyes flickered, and then he downed the rest of his coffee. "I have some supplies to pick up, and you have your own errands. I suggest we get going."

"Okay." She shot J.D. a sidelong glance as she gathered her jacket and bag. He seemed almost disappointed she didn't have any more traumas to share with him. Probably thought she was dull as dishwater.

"I'M TELLING YOU. She doesn't know anything." J.D. slammed the door of his truck and rested one arm on the steering wheel.

"Did she tell you about Abby?" Coburn's tone carried a challenge.

J.D. kept the sigh out of his voice. "No."

"Don't you think that's strange? She told you about the murder of her husband and yet she withholds the fact that her roommate took off without a trace. Why would she do that?"

"Maybe the D.C. cops did a good job of convincing her she had nothing to worry about. Noelle talked about traumatic events in her life. Obviously, the disappearance of a roommate doesn't rank up there with the murder of a spouse."

"How do we know she's not hiding something? How do we know Abby didn't confide in her? Give her the plans? Make her an accomplice?"

J.D. set his jaw. Coburn didn't get it. To him, Noelle was just another piece in a puzzle. Another suspicious person on the way to snagging Zendaris.

But to him— What was she to him?

"J.D.?" Coburn's voice sliced through his thoughts.

He had to protect Noelle. She didn't deserve any of this. He cleared his throat. "The subject would be safer if she knew and understood the threat facing her."

"The subject might be safer, but what about you? If she's involved and you tell her your interest in Zendaris, you've just overplayed your hand, putting yourself and this entire mission in jeopardy."

"She's not involved, Jack. I don't know why she hasn't told me about Abby, but it's not because she was Abby's accomplice." He thumped his chest. "I feel it."

"Feelings will get you in trouble."

"Better not let Lola hear you say that."

Coburn grunted. "I keep my feelings for my wife separate from the job."

"Wasn't always that way." Jack Coburn had met his wife when he'd been on the most important mission of his life—recovering his memory. And once the mission ended and he'd claimed Lola for his own, he'd never looked back and never had any regrets.

"I don't recommend it. The feelings I developed for Lola on that mission almost got me killed once or twice."

Coburn sucked in a breath. "You're not developing feelings for the subject, are you?"

Of course I am. He'd lost it the minute she'd turned those violet eyes on him.

"I'm not here just to track down any leads on Zendaris. I'm here to protect the subject, and I think she'd be safer knowing the truth."

"Unless that truth compromises your cover and our goal."

"I can't believe you'd sacrifice someone to reach Zendaris. That's not Prospero training."

"We don't have to throw Ms. Dupree to the wolves. You can protect her even if she doesn't know the truth—*that's* Prospero training."

"I'm doing my best, but I'm just the ranch hand. She's going to start getting suspicious once my mad spy skills become apparent."

"You'll figure it out, J.D. You always do."

"So the order to stay undercover still stands?"

"Until you can determine she's not part of Abby Warren's plot."

"That's exactly what I'm gonna do, boss."

Coburn ended the call, and J.D. checked the clock on the dash. He figured Noelle would be done with her errands before he was. He'd practically cleaned out the hardware store and checked out of his hotel.

He turned on the radio and tapped the steering wheel with his thumbs. He scanned the street for a white parka with a fur-trimmed hood. They were surprisingly popular, but none of the faces beneath the hoods were Noelle's—that combination of wariness and vulnerability.

Maybe he saw the vulnerability because he knew her past.

He grabbed the cell phone in the console and punched

the button for his contacts, realizing the moment he saw the empty list that he'd grabbed his secure Prospero phone.

He'd left the other phone in his coat pocket. He reached between the two front seats for his duster in the back. Pulling it into the front passenger seat, he fumbled for the pocket.

The phone fell on the floor of the truck, and he swore. Scooping it up, he glanced at the display. Noelle had texted him.

Took the shuttle to the mountain to meet Ted. You can leave or wait in town.

Dread thudded against his temples. He'd let her out of his sight, and she'd taken off to meet her brother. Hadn't he just proclaimed to Jack that his priority was protecting the subject?

He'd failed.

With thumbs suddenly too big for his phone's keyboard, he texted her back, asking why she'd gone to meet Ted.

He stared at the little display until his eyes burned and his mouth felt like sandpaper. When her response flashed on the screen, relief flooded his body, loosening the muscles he hadn't realized he'd been tensing.

He hurt himself snowboarding.

J.D. growled in the back of his throat. Why didn't Ted man up and stop running to his half sister every time he stubbed his toe?

Tired of the back-and-forth of little abbreviated words, J.D. punched the button to call Noelle's number.

She answered on the first ring and started talking. "You can go back to the house if you want. In case you didn't notice, I put a few purchases under the blue tarp in the back of your truck while you were still at the hardware store."

"I didn't notice, but you don't plan to get a ride to the house on the back of Ted's bike, do you? Is he in any condition to give you a ride?"

"I have no idea. I haven't found him yet."

J.D.'s heart slammed against his rib cage. "What do you mean? You haven't seen Ted yet?"

"I thought he'd be at the first-aid station here, but he's not and the ski patrol hasn't picked him up."

"Did he tell you he'd be at the first-aid station?"

"Actually, no. I just assumed. He texted me that he'd injured himself snowboarding and asked me to meet him on the mountain. When I tried texting him back, I didn't get a response. I tried calling and it went straight to an automated voice mail, like the phone was turned off. He may not be getting reception on the mountain, especially if he's on a run."

"Where are you now, Noelle?" His dry mouth seemed to be impeding his speech, and he didn't even know if his words had made sense.

"I'm still at the first-aid station. I figured if ski patrol picked him up, they'd bring him here."

"Stay there. Don't move. I'm on my way."

"J.D.? Are you okay?"

"I don't want to make you jumpy, but someone broke into your place—twice. He set up a camera the second time, and for all you know, the first time, too. I just don't like the idea of you roaming around the ski resort by yourself."

Her sharp intake of breath told him she hadn't even thought about her own safety as she'd run headlong to Ted's rescue.

"I-it's broad daylight. There are thousands of people crisscrossing this resort."

And Zendaris's men could still get to you if they wanted to.

"Just stay at the first-aid station. You're right. Ted will be headed there one way or another."

"Okay, I'm sitting down inside as we speak. You should be able to make it up here in fifteen minutes."

"I'm on my way—as we speak—so I'd better not drive and talk at the same time. Sit tight." He ended the call and tossed the phone into the cup holder.

The flurries had turned into some serious snowfall, so he cranked up the windshield wipers and the defroster. The snow on the road kept him from racing to the resort, but his hands clutched the steering wheel and his leg hovered over the gas pedal, aching to slam down the accelerator and go one hundred miles an hour to reach Noelle's side.

The slow-moving storm drew the skiers and boarders to the mountain like devotees on a pilgrimage—and that's what they were—snow devotees. He maneuvered his truck around the boarders clomping along in their boots and the skiers, their skis balanced on their shoulders, poles under their arms.

He waited for a car pulling out of a spot and glared at the other driver eyeing the same spot. The glare won, and J.D. pulled into the empty slot.

Breathless, feeling as if he'd just come down from the mountain himself, he strode toward the resort. He knew the first-aid station sat at the end of the row of windows selling passes and ski lessons, and he cut through the lines to reach the front door.

Pushing through the door, he spotted Noelle parked in a chair, her white jacket slung over her knees in the warm room. His jaw ached from tension, but he managed a smile and he also managed to not charge across the room, tuck her under one arm and haul her out of there.

"No sign of Ted?"

"It's weird. The patrol hasn't received any calls about an injured adult boarder matching Ted's description—only a few cocky teens and a newlywed trying to impress his wife."

"How long ago did Ted text you?" He held out his hand. "Can I see your phone?"

She fished in her bag and dropped her cell in his outstretched hand. "I've been sitting here for about twenty-five minutes, and it took me twenty minutes to get up here on the shuttle."

J.D. checked the time on the text, which matched Noelle's calculations. Then he noticed the sender, and he held up the phone facing her. "How do you know this text is from Ted?"

"Duh. The first thing in the text is *this is Ted.*"

"The sender is unknown. Don't you have his phone number in your contacts?"

She rolled her eyes. "Ted has trouble paying his bills sometimes. He usually goes with a prepaid phone."

"You said you reached voice mail. Was it his voice on the message?"

She crinkled her brow. "It was one of those recordings, you know, the caller you have reached, blah, blah."

He sat in the chair next to hers and placed the phone in her hand. Hadn't it occurred to her yet that the text could've come from anyone? Anyone who knew her half brother was in town. Anyone who knew she'd rush to his side. Anyone who knew Ted had an unidentifiable phone.

Anyone who knew a lot about Noelle Dupree.

"Have you tried calling him back since I talked to you?"

She pressed a button on the phone and listened. Then

she held it up to his ear. A robotic voice invited him to
leave a message at the tone.

"Do you know where Ted's staying?"

"He mentioned last night he'd met a few people at the
lodge up here. I'm assuming that means at the Buck Ridge
Lodge." She jerked a thumb over her shoulder. "It's that
way, where we're having dinner with Bruce tonight."

"I know it. Let's head over there."

Noelle waved to the attendant at the front desk. "Thanks
for your help. I guess my brother wasn't injured very seriously."

J.D. helped Noelle into her jacket, and she zipped it up
while they stepped into the cold. She flipped up the hood.
"I don't understand why all these people like skiing in
this mess. I'd rather wait until it clears up, leaving a nice
powdery carpet."

"There will be even more people when this storm
passes."

They trudged toward the Buck Ridge Lodge with its
timbered, Alpine roof and huge picture windows looking
out on the mountain. They swung through the red doors
in the front and wandered into the lobby.

Two steps down, the lobby opened onto an expansive
room with a fireplace in the center, its crackling blaze
drawing clutches of people around its perimeter.

One group held center court, beer bottles and coffee
mugs littering their table. And in the center of center
court—Ted Dupree—alive and well.

Noelle plucked at his sleeve. "That's Ted."

"I noticed."

She dragged him to the fireplace and nudged Ted in
the back with her knee. "What are you doing in here? Are
you okay?"

Ted turned and looked up at his sister with a flushed face. The fire or the booze?

"I told you I was staying up here with friends. I'm fine." He flicked his fingers at the scattered bottles. "It's coffee for me."

"Why is your phone off? Why didn't you let me know you were okay?"

Ted's dark brows collided over his nose.

J.D. held his breath.

"What are you talking about, girl? Why would I let you know I'm okay? I just saw you last night, and you sorta kicked me to the curb."

"B-but the call, the text." She fumbled for her phone and dropped it. It skidded beneath a table. "You texted me that you'd been injured."

"How could I do that? I don't even have a phone."

Chapter Nine

The room spun, and Noelle grabbed the back of Ted's over-stuffed chair. A trickle of sweat crawled down her back. "You didn't text me?"

"I just told you. I don't have a phone yet." He shoved a lock of black hair from his eyes and winked at the pretty redhead sitting across from him. "But I'd better remedy that situation."

"Ted!" She pushed the cushion of the chair against his back. Didn't he realize the importance of his statement? Her gaze darted to J.D.'s grim face. J.D. did.

Ted sprawled sideways in the chair so he could look at her without straining his neck. "What's wrong? I didn't get a phone yet. No big deal. I'll pick one up tomorrow and give you the number."

"I—I got a text from you." She sank to her knees and reached under the table for her cell, but J.D. beat her to it.

Her fingers brushed his beneath the table, and he gave hers a squeeze.

Straightening to his full height, he brought the phone with him. He stabbed at a few buttons and held the phone in front of Ted's face. "This didn't come from you?"

Ted squinted at the display, then turned to his friends. "Hey, did one of you play a trick on my sister and send her a text that I'd been injured on the slopes?"

The semicircle of people around Ted laughed and murmured but denied it.

"Weird." Ted shrugged. "Maybe there's another Ted in Buck Ridge. Weird coincidence. Speaking of weird coincidences. You'll never guess who I saw in this very hotel."

"Bruce Pierpont."

Ted snapped his fingers. "Maybe he texted you as a practical joke, even though that dude doesn't have much of a sense of humor."

Reaching behind, Noelle pulled herself onto the ledge of the fireplace. "That's it."

Ted lost interest in the little drama and had turned back to his new friends, but J.D. joined her on the fireplace, scooting her over with his hip.

"Do you think it could've been Pierpont?" He held the cell phone out to her, pinched between two fingers as if it were toxic.

"Maybe he didn't do it as a practical joke. Maybe he saw Ted here and figured it was a way to lure me up to the resort alone."

"Why would he want to do that?" J.D. hunched forward, elbows on his knees. "And how'd he know you'd come alone?"

"I don't know, J.D. I'm just grasping at straws here." She worried her bottom lip between her teeth. She didn't know what to think. Why would Bruce or anyone else want to get her up the mountain, with or without J.D. in tow?

"Don't you have Bruce's phone number?"

The fire had slowly been heating her back through the downy feathers of her jacket, and her mouth felt parched. She tugged off her jacket and let it slip to the floor.

"I do have his number." With stiff, clammy fingers she scrolled through her contacts until she reached Bruce's number. If he had called her from his cell phone, his name would've popped up on the display. It hadn't.

They both stared at the phone in her hand. J.D. finally broke the suffocating silence. "Do you want to call him to see if he still has the same number?"

"I suppose so." She curled her hand around the phone and squeezed it. Then she selected Bruce's name from her contacts and called it.

His voice mail picked up, and the phone almost slid from Noelle's grasp. "I-it's Noelle. Just confirming for dinner tonight. Seven o'clock."

"The old number still works?" J.D. asked once she'd hung up.

She nodded. "Unless he has two cell phones, that text didn't come from Bruce."

"Maybe Sheriff Greavy can ping the phone."

"Do you really think the person who texted me to lure me up here for some reason is going to use a phone that can be traced or *pinged,* whatever that is?"

"No." The palm of his hand rubbed a circle on her back. "That's why you need to be careful. No more running to anyone's rescue without thinking it through first—or without notifying me."

"I thought you were helping me with the ranch, not becoming my personal bodyguard." Although the thought of a personal bodyguard right now put a warm glow around her heart—especially a personal bodyguard like J.D. For some reason, he really did care what happened to her.

Probably didn't want to come back to the ranch to find his employer, landlord and all-around benefactor dead.

Dead? Why would someone want her dead? Why would someone break into her apartment in D.C. and then follow her to Colorado and break into her ranch house? Then lure her to the mountain under false pretenses?

She buried her face in her hands.

The pressure of J.D.'s hand increased and the circles became caresses. "If someone really wanted to hurt you, he would've done it by now. He's had a few opportunities. He had access to your place in D.C. He could've hidden out there and waited for you."

She splayed her fingers and peered at him through the spaces. "Is that supposed to make me feel safer?"

He tugged on the ends of her hair. "I'm looking at it from a practical standpoint here. Whoever this is wants something from you. He's looking for something."

"He's got the wrong Noelle Dupree. I don't have anything that anyone could possibly want."

"I wouldn't say that." His fingers sifted through her hair as if testing the weight of each strand.

She held still, hunched forward, her breath coming in short spurts. She didn't want to move, afraid to break the connection between them. Closing her eyes, she leaned into his touch—just a little.

"Did you figure out the phone thing?" Ted had twisted in his chair during a break in the lively conversation.

Noelle jerked back, and J.D.'s magic touch disappeared.

"It was just some weird coincidence." She didn't feel like giving Ted any of the details of her crazy life, not when he was on the path to sobriety.

"So, since you didn't come up here to see me, I'm going to crash in my friends' room for a while." He leaned over the arm of his chair and kissed her cheek. "See you later, J.D. No hard feelings about you staying at the guesthouse. I found better digs."

Ted pushed out of his chair and draped an arm around the redhead as they ventured across the lobby.

"Your brother's a player."

"That's how he's managed to stay alive all these years—sheer charm."

"Must run in the family." He bumped her with his shoulder.

Was he kidding? She was about as lacking in charm these days as that soggy mitten crumpled on the floor.

Clearing his throat, J.D. rose from the fireplace and held out his hand to her. "What's the story with him, if you don't mind my asking? He doesn't look much older than you. Did your father have a relationship before he married your mother?"

When she got to her feet, she snatched her hand away from his. "Actually, Ted's my younger brother."

"Oops, sorry, didn't mean to pry." He hunched his shoulders in his black duster, which made them look even broader.

She waved her hand to dismiss the past. "It's old news. My father committed an...indiscretion a few years into the marriage with my mother."

And who could blame him? Her mother had been a controlling neat freak who'd hated life on the ranch. Mom had driven her to make her own bad marriage just so she could get out of the house.

Noelle clenched her jaw. Her marriage to Alex hadn't been all bad. They could've worked things out.

"What about Ted's mother?" J.D. had placed his hand on the small of her back and was steering her through the skiers and boarders as they headed to the lodge's après-ski.

"Let's just say Ted inherited his predilection for drugs and alcohol from her." In fact, Ted's mother had been the polar opposite of Noelle's.

"Sounds like a soap opera."

"Just life, I guess." She stopped on the wide stone steps in front of the lodge and grabbed J.D.'s arm. "Good job."

"Huh?"

"Good job distracting me from the fact that some stranger lured me up here on false pretenses for God knows what."

Pinching her chin between his thumb and index finger, he tilted back her head. "Nothing we can do about it right now. Let's go back to the ranch and get ready for dinner with Pierpont. Maybe we can get something out of him. Whether or not we do, I'm not letting you out of my sight."

She sighed. That sounded too good to be true.

HOW THE HELL had Zendaris's guys known about Ted and Noelle's tendency to rush to his rescue? How'd they know she'd go alone to the ski resort? Maybe they were just throwing tactics against the wall like strands of spaghetti to see what stuck.

More to the point, what had they planned to do with her once they got her alone? He knew they wouldn't harm her—at least not right away. They wanted to find out what she knew about Abby first.

Hell, *he* wanted to find out what she knew about Abby.

Pushing back his damp hair, he inspected his teeth in the mirror. If he planned to go up against Bruce Chandler Pierpont the Third, he'd better not have any spinach between his teeth.

He slammed the door of the guesthouse and climbed into his truck. Seemed kind of dumb to pick up his date when she lived a stone's throw away, but he cranked on the engine and rolled the truck across the yard to the ranch house anyway.

He hopped out of the truck and strode toward the house, but Noelle stopped him when she floated onto the porch dressed in a pair of skinny jeans and furry boots with a Russian-style hat topping her glossy black hair.

"You look…Russian." He shoved his hands in his pockets and swallowed. What an idiotic thing to say. He'd been ready to pay her another compliment, but she didn't seem to like his compliments.

She patted the sides of the hat with both hands. "This? I bought it the last time I was in New York."

He opened the door of the truck for her and gave her a hand in.

He avoided the subject of the break-ins and the text, and Noelle didn't seem to want to bring them up either. They could be going on a regular date except for the menace that overshadowed them…and Noelle had no idea who he really was. Other than all that—regular date.

But this wasn't a regular date. He took a deep breath. "Did Pierpont call you back after you left him that message?"

"Yes." She pulled on her gloves as he swung the car into the resort parking lot, sparser than earlier in the day, but still populated with the vehicles of night skiers and lodge guests.

"Did his name appear on your display when he called you back?" He threw the car into Park, and she didn't wait for him to get the door. Didn't answer him either.

He scrambled from the truck and circled to the passenger side. "Well?"

He took her arm to cross the slick asphalt and felt her shiver beneath her coat.

"Yep, same number. Like I said, unless he has a different cell phone, he didn't send me that text."

"Let's see if we can find out why old Bruce followed you to Colorado." He entwined his fingers with hers as they walked up the expansive steps of the Buck Ridge Lodge.

If she didn't want Pierpont making moves on her, he'd

make sure that didn't happen—not that protecting her from unwanted male attention fell into his job description.

Guests packed the lobby lounge area, sipping hot drinks and sharing pitchers of beer, all gravitating toward the blazing warmth in the fireplace. No sign of Ted and his companions this time.

They crossed the lobby and descended a flight of stairs to the restaurant. Low voices and clinking silverware hinted at a different atmosphere down here. Definitely more Pierpont's style than the rabble upstairs.

"Table for two?" The hostess smiled, pencil poised above her book.

"Actually, we're meeting someone—Pierpont?" J.D. tugged off his gloves and shoved them in his pockets. He wanted to grab Noelle's hand again but after removing her own gloves, she'd left her hands in her pockets.

"He's already here." The hostess dropped her pencil and led them past a bar into the main dining room.

Pierpont spied their approach and rose in greeting. "Coat hooks on the other side of the booth. That hat suits you, Noelle."

"Thanks." She took it off her head and shook out her hair.

J.D. helped her with her coat before Pierpont could get his hands on her, and he hung it up next to his.

She scooted into the booth across from Pierpont, and J.D. slid in after her.

Pierpont tapped the wine list. "I took the liberty of ordering a bottle of wine for the table. Do you drink wine, J.D.?"

"On occasion."

"Bruce not only collects art, he's also a connoisseur of fine wines." Noelle flicked her napkin onto her lap.

"That's comforting." J.D. couldn't care less about fine

wines, or fine art for that matter, although he was sure he'd like whatever kind of art Noelle created, starting with that picture in the living room at the ranch house.

Pierpont gave him a tight smile. "What does J.D. stand for? I don't think I caught your last name."

"Jim Davis, but everybody calls me J.D."

"That's…convenient."

"Convenient?"

"Initials—I guess BCP, my initials, just don't have the same ring to them as J.D."

J.D. shrugged and tipped his chin at the waiter hovering at their table, showing a wine label to Pierpont. "Is that our fine wine?"

Pierpont studied the label as if the waiter was trying to pull a fast one on him.

"Perfect."

The waiter poured a thimbleful into Pierpont's glass. He swirled it around and sniffed it, closing his eyes.

With Pierpont's eyes closed, J.D. took the opportunity to nudge Noelle in the side. She rewarded him with a kick under the table.

Pierpont finally sipped the ruby liquid and then proceeded to swish it around in his mouth.

J.D. coughed, trying to choke back a laugh, and this time Noelle pinched his thigh. He liked that a lot better than the kick and squeezed her knee back.

The ritual over, Pierpont swallowed and nodded his approval to the waiter.

As the waiter filled Noelle's glass first, J.D. said, "Whew—for a minute there I thought you were going to start gargling with it."

Noelle snorted and the waiter's hand trembled just a little before he started pouring some of the wine into J.D.'s proffered glass.

"That's how it's done, J.D." Pierpont spread his delicate-looking hands.

The guy had probably never done a lick of manual labor in his life.

The waiter left the bottle, and Pierpont pinched the stem of his glass between two fingers. "What branch of the service were you in?"

J.D. had the wineglass halfway to his lips but set it down so that the liquid sloshed against the sides. "I don't recall mentioning I was in the service."

"You didn't. It's your bearing, certainly not your hair-cut." Pierpont chuckled. "Living in D.C. for as long as I did, you see a lot of military. I recognize the stance."

Pierpont's eyes turned stony above the fake smile.

This guy was more on the ball than he'd figured. He needed to tread lightly—as much fun as it was to antagonize Bruce Chandler Pierpont the Third.

If Pierpont, with all his resources, started investigating J.D.'s background, he'd definitely have some explaining to do to Noelle. Time for some damage control.

J.D. brought the glass to his lips and sipped. He closed his eyes and murmured, "Ahhh. That's good. You really do know your wine, Bruce."

Pierpont spun the bottle around so the label faced J.D. "It's an Australian Shiraz—perfect for appetizers."

"Then let's order some." J.D. skimmed his fingertip up the one-page menu printed just that day and recited each overpriced appetizer on the menu. "Anything sound good?"

"It all sounds good." Noelle turned her head to stare at him, her brows raised.

"Are you a connoisseur of fine food, too, Bruce?"

"Yes." Pierpont narrowed his eyes, waiting for the punch line, no doubt.

J.D. didn't have one. He sniffed his wine; the fruity aroma was as intoxicating as the taste. "If you can pick food like you pick wine, we leave it up to you to choose something to go with this Shiraz. Right, Noelle?"

"Um, sure." She nudged him again with the toe of her boot, but she'd have to pinch him again if she wanted his attention.

"Well, then." Pierpont straightened up in his seat and shook out his menu, bringing it close to the candle flickering on the table. "Let's see what they have to offer."

When the waiter returned, Pierpont rattled off a bunch of choices, but all J.D. heard was *oysters,* which he detested.

When the appetizers arrived, J.D. ignored the flip-flop of his gut and prepared for his next assault on Pierpont to preoccupy his attention.

He dropped another oyster on his plate and snapped his fingers. "Pierpont—banking, right?"

"Steel." Pierpont slurped from a shell.

J.D. gulped some water to keep from gagging. "Was that your grandfather? Great-grandfather?"

That set Pierpont off just like J.D. had known it would. If there was one thing his rich buddy, Gage, had taught him, it was that the wealthy, especially old wealth, enjoyed talking about their money and how they got it. Pierpont proved to be no exception.

As Pierpont rambled on about his family's money and interests, they ordered their food, and J.D. got a steak to erase the fishy taste of the oysters.

By the time the waiter returned to take their dessert order, Noelle put her foot down, both figuratively and literally as her heel ground into the toe of J.D.'s boot before he could ask Pierpont another question.

"I don't think Bruce is an expert on desserts, so I'll take the key lime pie, please."

J.D. jerked his thumb toward Noelle. "I'll have some of her pie and a coffee, please."

After Pierpont put in his order, he excused himself to use the men's room.

When he turned the corner toward the stairs, Noelle turned on him. "What are you doing?"

"Finding out about Pierpont."

"So run him through a search engine or ask me. I already know all this stuff about his family—*ad nauseum.* Once you get him wound up, you can't turn him off."

"I'm trying to get a measure of the man, see if he's the stalking type." *And make sure he doesn't unearth my identity.*

"How is learning about his great-grandfather's investment in steel mills doing that?"

"You never know. People slip up."

"You know what?" She held up her hands. "I thought you were good at this spy stuff. Now I have serious doubts. I want to find out what he's doing here. He's never fully explained that."

The waiter delivered their coffee. "The desserts will be right up. Would you like two forks for that key lime pie?"

"Please."

Pierpont returned before they could continue their discussion. He tipped some cream into his coffee cup. "And what about you, J.D.? Your family's in ranching?"

Noelle tapped her spoon on the side of her water glass. "I hate to break up this little bromance, but I'd like some answers of my own, Bruce."

Atta girl, Noelle.

Pierpont looked up from swirling the cream into his coffee in what looked like a perfect spiral. "Really?"

"Yes, really. Why did you follow me out to Colorado?"

"I thought we discussed this. I was in the market for a ski vacation and your presence in Buck Ridge seemed fortuitous."

"Why is my presence necessary for your ski vacation?"

"Just because Alex left us doesn't mean I'm any less interested in helping you turn that guesthouse into a studio. That's one investment I'd like to make."

"And I thought we discussed *this* before. I don't need your help to turn it into a studio."

"I know. I know." Pierpont paused as the waiter put the two desserts on the table. "The money you got from Alex's life insurance should be put aside as a nest egg or invested. You shouldn't use it for the studio."

Noelle clutched her fork, the knuckles of her hand turning white. "It seems right."

Sighing, Pierpont sliced a neat triangle off his piece of fudge cake. "Guilt."

Noelle's hand jerked and her water glass tipped over, soaking the white tablecloth. She tossed her napkin on top of the stain. "Excuse me, J.D. I'm going to use the ladies' room."

J.D. rose from the booth, and as Noelle squeezed past him, a tear glistening on her cheek caught the low lights of the restaurant.

Pierpont didn't seem to notice as he surgically removed another bite of cake from the slice in front of him.

Noelle hadn't touched the key lime pie before she stormed off, and it didn't seem right to start without her. J.D. folded his arms on the table. "What did you mean—guilt?"

"When Alex got murdered, Noelle collected his life insurance, but she hasn't spent a penny of it in two years. I assume it's because she feels guilty."

J.D. knew all the facts about Noelle's life but none of the emotion that went along with those facts. "You mean like survivor's guilt? 'Why him and not me?'"

"Not—" Pierpont balanced the tines of his fork on the edge of his plate "—really."

"She can't believe she could've stopped the murder."

"Not that either."

J.D. was ready to punch Pierpont in the face if he didn't get to the point. He uncrossed his arms and leaned back against the seat. "Are you going to tell me or what?"

"She felt guilty because she didn't love Alex anymore."

J.D. schooled his face into neutral lines. Pierpont's words surprised him, but he wouldn't give the weasel the satisfaction of knowing that. "How do you know all this?"

"I was there." Pierpont resumed his dismantling of the cake. "I saw how it was."

"How was it?" If Pierpont tried to tell him Noelle loved him instead, he *would* punch him in the face.

"I was friends with both of them. Alex started out with a bang, but Noelle's star started to surpass his. Her art was getting more attention, and Alex responded like the petulant boy he was."

"He took out his frustration on her?"

"Yes." Pierpont popped the last morsel of cake into his mouth.

"Not physically?" J.D.'s hands bunched into fists under the table.

"Nothing like that, but he started getting controlling— watching her every move, monitoring her emails, texts, following her to work. It drove her nuts, especially after escaping from that mother of hers."

Mother? J.D. knew nothing about Noelle except the facts and figures on paper. Her mother lived in Arizona with a sister. Come to think of it, she and her mother must be estranged if she didn't go to her for comfort.

"So she fell out of love with him."

"If you ask me, she never did love him, but this new side of sweet Alex put the nail in the coffin—so to speak. She asked him for a divorce, and he refused. That was the state of their relationship when someone pumped a few bullets into Alex."

Noelle emerged from around the corner, and J.D. cleared his throat.

Pierpont stabbed his fork in the air above the key lime pie. "Are you going to eat this?"

Noelle hovered at the table, her eyes slits. "Still getting to know each other?"

"I've been drooling over this pie waiting for you to get back." J.D. stood up to let her back in the booth.

"You could've started without me." She waved her napkin at Pierpont. "Didn't seem to bother Mr. Etiquette to start without me. And finish without me."

"Was that bad manners? I really didn't think you were going to eat it, my dear."

"I am." Noelle stabbed the fork into the pie, demolishing the perfect dab of whipped cream in the center in the process. She stuffed a huge piece in her mouth, her violet eyes tracking between him and Pierpont while she chewed.

J.D. claimed his own forkful before she laid siege to the whole piece.

Pierpont wrinkled his nose. "Glad to see you got your appetite back after marching off in a huff. I only spoke the truth. You have no reason to feel guilty about Alex's death or spending his life-insurance money, if that's what you want to do."

"Cut it." Noelle drew the fork across her throat, looking as if she'd like to be holding it against Pierpont's.

She and Pierpont patched things up over coffee as they discussed plans for the studio. Noelle might not want Pierpont's money for the project, but she didn't mind his ideas.

At the end of the meal, Pierpont grabbed for the check and scribbled on it, charging the meal to his room. "I insist. If you won't let me fund the studio project, I can at least buy you dinner."

"Thanks, Bruce. We'd better get going. Buck Ridge is expecting even heavier snowfall tonight."

"Are you sure you two don't want a nightcap? If you're going to become a wine snob, you'll have to drink more than two glasses, J.D."

"Another time—not when I have to drive down the mountain." J.D. snatched the coats from the hook and helped Noelle into hers.

He'd tried to keep his wits sharp, but Pierpont didn't have the same goal. He'd consumed another bottle of wine, mostly on his own, and the hard questioning attitude he'd brought to the table had disappeared in direct proportion to the wine.

J.D. planned to avoid these little get-togethers in the future. Pierpont would get nothing from him. Not until J.D. was ready to come clean to Noelle on his own.

Pierpont walked them out as far as the lobby and then retreated to the lounge for that nightcap.

The icy wind slapped J.D. in the face, and his eyes watered. He drew the brim of his hat lower over his forehead.

"Ooh." Noelle's word formed in the air. "It's cold."

"Better pull that Russian getup of yours over your ears." He turned toward her and tugged the bottom of her hat toward her chin.

Then he kissed her, cold lips against cold lips, but it lit a fire in his belly. He could always blame it on the Shiraz. Still gripping her hat, he pulled her even closer, his mouth warming to the task. The tip of her freezing nose jabbed his cheek. Then her elbow jabbed his midsection—and the fire went out.

"Whoa. Maybe this isn't a good idea."

Seemed like a great idea one minute ago. "Sorry. Two glasses of wine and I turn into a slut."

She giggled, which stoked the embers again. He'd never heard her giggle before.

"Let's get out of this miserable weather." He put his arm around her waist to guide her to the truck, and she didn't jab him with anything else.

With Noelle snug beside him, J.D. started the engine and got down to the business of getting them safely back to the ranch.

The road down the mountain had a few twists and turns, but his four-wheel-drive vehicle hugged the icy asphalt. Their dinner with Pierpont had run late, and they had to share the road with only a few other cars.

A pair of headlights glared behind him, and he adjusted his rearview mirror. "Must be some idiot who doesn't realize you don't use your brights in the snow."

Noelle yawned. "There are a lot of idiots like that out here during ski season."

The headlights pressed on. Bigger. Brighter.

J.D. licked his lips and glanced at the speedometer. *Nope. Not going any faster.*

On the next straightaway, J.D. pulled the truck to the right, flirting with the shoulder. If this maniac wanted to pass him, he could give it a try.

The car stuck with him and followed him into the curve. J.D.'s tires fishtailed a little on the ice, and he eased off the accelerator.

"Whoa." Noelle grabbed the edge of her seat. "I think the plows better get out here."

The car loomed behind them, but J.D. kept his speed steady. Maybe the driver had been drinking at the lodge—even more reason for him to slow down.

The snow flurries created a white sheet over the windshield, so J.D. took the next turn even slower. He could see the headlights of the other car closing in, but he couldn't even make out the car itself.

The truck jolted and skidded toward the edge of the mountain road.

Noelle yelped. "What was that?"

Before J.D. could respond, the car behind them smashed into their bumper again.

"What's going on?"

"A car ran into us—twice, but we can't pull off here. I can't even see where the road ends and the drop-off begins."

The headlights behind them disappeared. J.D. said, "Did he go off the road?"

The next assault came from the driver's side, as the rogue car bashed into the truck's side bumper. The force of the hit sent the truck into a spin on the icy road.

Noelle screamed.

J.D. fought to control the wheel, steering into the skid. Metal on metal screeched as the passenger side of the truck raked the guardrail.

The truck lurched forward and plowed into something solid. The air bags deployed with a thump, and the truck screamed to a halt.

"Are you okay, Noelle?" He cranked his head to the side, his cheek scraping the air bag. "Noelle?"

The air bag had Noelle pinned to the seat, but her body was slumped to the side, her head against the cracked window.

"Noelle?" J.D. reached across the seat, and her head fell back, a trickle of blood oozing from her temple.

"If she doesn't come out of this, Zendaris, you're a dead man."

Chapter Ten

The voices were coming back. They had faded away, and now they murmured and swirled around her, just like the snow. She stuck out her tongue to catch some.

"Noelle?" Warm fingers pressed her cheek, and she inhaled the distinctly masculine scent of J.D. "She's awake."

"How's your head feeling, Noelle?"

Her head? Blinking, she reached up, her fingers stumbling across a bandage. Her temple throbbed beneath it, and she closed her eyes. The darkness behind her lids soothed her.

The accident.

She struggled to sit up, but firm hands patted her back down. "It's okay. We're going to load you into the ambulance now."

"J-J.D.?" She chattered out the name, a sudden chill seizing her neck and jaw.

A gloved hand grabbed hers. "I'm right here. I'm riding in the ambulance with you."

Her world jerked and swayed, and she squeezed her eyes shut tighter, but they were just rolling her stretcher to the ambulance.

The ride to the hospital was a blur of the EMT asking her questions about the day of the week and the president in between pokes and prods from various medical instruments. And J.D. Always J.D., murmuring soothing words, touching her hand and adjusting the sheet covering her body.

As long as they didn't pull that sheet over her face, she figured she was okay.

Later, it could've been minutes, it could've been hours, her stretcher zoomed through the emergency entrance to the hospital and down a shiny corridor that resembled more snow.

She was still woozy and a little nauseous, but she was able to answer the doctor's questions, and she remembered the accident itself up until the point where the truck hit the guardrail. That's when she must've smacked her head against the car window.

She even remembered floating in and out of consciousness as J.D. pulled her from the car and the sirens from the ambulance wailed to the rescue.

When she got back to her room after the CAT scan, J.D. crept in and pulled up a chair.

She opened one eye. "Concussion—nothing more."

"That's enough. You had me going there for a while. You'd come to and then check out. Scared the hell out of me."

"How are you?"

"I'm fine." He rolled up his sleeves and held up his arms, bent at the elbow. "Just some abrasions from the air bag."

"The other car?"

"Took off."

"What? Like a hit-and-run? Because it was totally his fault, unless he was skidding. But then, why take off?"

J.D. shifted his gaze downward, his thick, dark lashes dropping. "I don't think it was an accident, Noelle."

"You mean he was drunk, or…" The nausea hit her again and she gagged.

"Water?" J.D.'s hand hovered over the plastic pitcher next to her bed.

She nodded, her eyes never leaving his, although he avoided her stare.

He handed her the cup, and she took a sip. Then she wiped the back of her hand across her mouth.

"You mean someone tried to run us off the road on purpose, don't you?"

"After all that's happened, it's too much of a coincidence to believe otherwise. If the other car's brakes failed or it hit an icy patch, why would the driver take off after we crashed?"

"Maybe he'd been drinking and was afraid he'd get cited for a DUI." She pleated the sheet with shaky fingers. She didn't want to be having this conversation.

"If he was drinking and driving, he would've stopped the first time he bumped us."

Crumpling the sheet in her fist, she said, "But why? Why would someone stalking me want to kill us?"

"Incapacitate."

"Excuse me?"

"I don't know that bumping a car like that into a guardrail would kill the occupants of the car, but it would incapacitate us. It knocked you out."

"But why? It doesn't make any sense to me."

J.D. jumped up from the plastic chair so quickly it tipped over and fell to the floor, bouncing once. He paced to the window, plowing his fingers through his hair.

The frustration emanated from his body in waves, so palpable she could feel it washing over her, merging with her own frustration into a crescendo ready to crash and engulf them both.

Throughout the chaos of the past few days, it comforted her to know that J.D. had taken on her problems as his own. He wanted to nail her stalker as much as she did.

And he'd kissed her. His interest in her had surpassed the mystery of the break-in and the text message. Or maybe the danger had been drawing them closer. She didn't mind, although that kind of immediate attraction posed a danger all its own.

He continued staring out the window, lost in his own thoughts.

She coughed. "If they wanted to incapacitate us, they were successful. So why did they force us off the road and then leave?"

"They didn't leave—not right away."

J.D. rubbed his chin with his knuckles, and she held her breath, which caused her head to pound even more.

"A patrol car happened to be following us some distance back. He drove up on the scene, saw my truck smashed against the boulder by the guardrail and saw another car, emergency lights flashing, pulled over ahead of us."

"They *did* pull over." She expelled the breath with her words.

"The cop could make out a figure approaching through the snow flurries and called out. He expected the person to follow him to the accident, but as the officer reached us, he heard an engine and the car took off."

Noelle shivered and pulled the hospital sheet up to her chin. "The person who bumped us was coming to see his handiwork and then took off when he saw the patrol car."

"Seems like it.

"It could still mean the driver had been drinking and wanted to see how we were but didn't want the cop to find him out."

"Maybe." J.D. wandered back to the window and wedged his shoulder on the wall next to it.

"You don't believe that, do you? What's your take?"

"It's like you said before. The driver ran us off the road and was coming back to see his handiwork."

"And then what?" Her fingertips traced the bump forming above her temple. "You said you didn't think he wanted to kill us, just incapacitate us. So why did he come back?"

"To take you."

Noelle gasped. J.D.'s words were like a punch to the gut.

He reached her bed in two strides, straightened the up-ended chair and straddled it. "I'm sorry to scare you, Noelle, but that's what I think. This person doesn't want to kill you. He wants something from you."

"He wants to kidnap me?" She drew her knees to her chest, wrapping her arms around her legs. "Why are you so sure about this, J.D.?"

He reached back and squeezed his neck, tilting back his head and closing his eyes. "All signs point to it. He could've killed you if he wanted. That's not what he wants."

"Well, I don't know what he wants. Maybe he should just ask me."

"Are you sure you don't know? Nothing else unusual has occurred recently?"

Noelle bit her lip as Abby's disappearance flitted across her mind again. Did this have anything to do with her secretive roommate? "Maybe…"

"Yes?" J.D. hunched forward in his chair.

"Maybe this is somehow connected to my roommate in D.C."

"It's late." The nurse charged into the room with a chart and a tray of bandages. "You need to leave now, sir. Visiting hours are over, and we need to change Noelle's bandage and check a few vitals. You can come back first thing tomorrow morning."

J.D. looked ready to knock the tray from the nurse's hands. "A few more minutes?"

"I'm afraid not. In fact, it's past visiting hours and we need to give this young lady the once-over before she gets some sleep."

"We'll talk tomorrow." Noelle pressed her fingertips against her forehead as another wave of pain and cloudiness suffused her head. The accident jarred through her memory again, and she clutched the side rails of the bed.

"Are you all right?" J.D. scooted his chair closer and smoothed his thumb across the back of her hand.

The nurse clicked her tongue. "That's what I'm talking about. She needs to rest."

"I'll be back first thing tomorrow. I'm going to get a hotel room in town." He leaned over the bed and kissed the edge of her bandage.

She nodded, already wishing him gone.

Words. Words came at her from all sides. Abby's words. Ted's words. Bruce's words. J.D.'s words—soothing, comforting.

Angry.

J.D. POUNDED HIS fist against the wall of his hotel room. "Damn it, Jack. She doesn't know anything about Zendaris. Before I left her hospital room tonight, she was ready to tell me about Abby. She wouldn't do that if she had something to hide."

"She's all right now?"

"She's fine." He pinched the bridge of his nose. "If you call sustaining a concussion fine."

"And you?"

"I'm touched by your concern, boss, but I've got bigger issues here. Zendaris just stepped it up tonight. His men went after Noelle with me in the car."

"They were going after you, too, J.D., whether or not they realize you're Prospero. It's enough that you're protecting this woman. You're in the way."

"You're probably right, but that just makes the situation that much more dangerous for Noelle. She deserves to know who's after her. Who knows? She might be able to give us info about Abby that we don't know."

"You already said Noelle doesn't know anything—either she does or she doesn't."

J.D. clenched his fist and eyed the wall again, but he passed this time. "She doesn't consciously know anything. She would've brought it up if she did. But unconsciously? Maybe once I tell her the whole story about Abby, it will jog her memory. We should've trusted her from the get-go."

Jack cleared his throat. "Prospero doesn't trust anyone from the get-go. Look at what happened with Colonel Scripps. Sometimes we can't even trust our own."

"Prospero's different under you, Jack. I'd trust any one of you with my life."

"Stop trying to kiss my ass. If you're sure about this woman, then go for it. We haven't turned up anything suspicious on her after all our digging."

"Thank you!" J.D. pumped his fist in the air. "She just might lead us to the missing plans."

"Maybe, but once she finds out an international arms dealer without a shred of scruples is after her, she may never let you out of her sight."

J.D. dropped onto the bed. That prospect didn't sound half-bad. "You don't know this woman, Jack. She doesn't back down."

"It's your job to make sure she does. We don't need to leave a trail of dead civilians on our quest to nail Zendaris."

"That's not going to happen. I'll protect Noelle with my life."

J.D. could hear Coburn sigh over the line.

"I—I mean, I'd protect any civilian against Zendaris with my life."

"Yeah, yeah. I know that. Watch your back. Zendaris's guys have the advantage."

"They do?"

"They have their sights trained on you…and you don't have a clue what they even look like."

J.D. tossed the phone onto the nightstand and stretched out on the bed, his boots hanging off the edge. He couldn't wait to come clean to Noelle tomorrow morning. They'd work this together, and knowing the source of the threats against her would keep her safer.

He could finally tell her his true identity. Would she like J.D. the spy better than she liked J.D. the ranch hand? Would she trust that J.D. more? Let him get closer?

He'd have his answer soon enough.

The following morning, J.D. left his hotel for a brisk walk to the hospital a block away. He'd already arranged to have a rental car delivered to the hospital. Between that guardrail and the boulder, his truck was totaled.

He stopped along the way for a couple of lattes and a blueberry scone in case Noelle couldn't stomach the hospital breakfast.

Riding up the elevator to the fourth floor, he whistled a tuneless series of notes. He waved to the nurses at the front station and headed down the antiseptic-smelling corridor to Noelle's room, his boots scuffing against the shiny linoleum.

The door stood open, and he poked his head around the corner, into the room. The doctor had a penlight out, shining it in Noelle's eyes.

J.D.'s heart skipped a beat or two. "Everything okay, Doctor?"

The doctor turned and flashed the beam of light onto an X-ray. "Sharing the good news with Noelle. She definitely had a concussion, but the CAT scan doesn't show any cracks to the skull. She's free to go today."

"That's great." J.D. shifted his gaze to Noelle's face, where the good news hadn't registered. He held up the coffees, the bag of goodies clutched in his right hand. "I brought you a latte and scone from the coffeehouse down the street."

"Thanks." Her lips barely moved as she eked out the word.

J.D. raised his brows. "Did you have a good night's sleep? Is your head still bothering you?"

"Ibuprofen dulls the pain, and as long as I didn't crack my skull, I'm thrilled."

She didn't look thrilled—not at all. "Any instructions before I take her home, Doc?"

"The nurse will review some instructions with you." The doctor slid the X-ray films from the light board. "Do you two live together?"

"No." Noelle practically shouted the denial. "He stays in the guesthouse."

The way she said *guesthouse,* it might've been *doghouse.* The pain must be getting to her, or she wasn't herself yet. The nurse would probably explain more.

The doctor's eyebrows shot up to his nonexistent hairline. "Your friend is going to have to keep an eye on you today—just today. You should be fine, but keep taking the ibuprofen for the pain as well as the swelling."

The doctor left the room with a wave of Noelle's file.

J.D. sat in the chair by the bed, placing the coffees on the bedside table. "Did you have breakfast already?"

Her eyes, more violet than ever, bored into him, and he flinched from the intensity. Had the concussion messed with her mind?

He wrapped his fingers around one of the coffee cups and presented it to her while taking a sip from his own.

Her hand shot out and cinched his wrist so hard he almost dropped the latte.

"Who the hell is Zendaris?"

Chapter Eleven

J.D.—or whoever he was—choked on his coffee. *Good.* He deserved much worse for lying to her, keeping things from her, trying to control her. She'd had enough of that to last a lifetime.

"Well?" She whipped the sheet off and swung her legs over the side of the hospital bed, planting her feet on the floor. "Who is Zendaris?"

He placed his coffee cup on the table next to hers and brushed his hands together. "Where did you hear that name?"

"From your own lips." Those lips that had felt so warm and inviting against her own. Those lying lips.

He tilted his head, and a lock of tawny hair fell across his forehead. Even liars could look sexy.

"When did I mention Zendaris?"

"Right after the crash last night. You must've thought I was unconscious, but I wasn't—not yet. I heard you blame Zendaris for the accident."

She'd also remembered his vow to kill Zendaris if anything happened to her. But that didn't erase his deception. Who the hell was he, anyway? Why had he finagled his way into her life? Into her heart? And why had she let him?

That almost cut deeper. He'd been playing up to her, coming on to her, making her believe they had some emotional connection. And all this time he'd been leading her on for some nefarious reason—because he had *nefarious* written all over his handsome face.

He blew out a breath on a whistle. "You heard that, huh?"

"I heard it but didn't remember until last night after you'd left. I thought I may have imagined it since the voices in my head were coming fast and furious, but everything I heard had actually happened. I wasn't dreaming or hallucinating. Besides, why would I come up with a name like Zendaris?"

"Not a very likely name to dream up out of thin air, I agree."

"Stop stalling." She stamped her foot on the cold linoleum. "Who is he, and why would he be after me? And more to the point, who are you?"

"My name is J.D." He spread his hands in supplication. "That's not a lie."

But everything else was? Including those intimate looks, the kisses, those soothing touches?

She grabbed a pillow and threw it at him. He ducked, deflecting it with his hands, and it hit the bedside table. One foamy latte keeled over.

Picking up the cup, he said, "Whoa. I'm going to tell you everything. In fact—" he licked his fingers "—I was going to tell you everything this morning, even though I'm sure you don't believe me now."

"You're right."

The nurse bustled into the room. "I brought your release forms. Is this strong guy gonna take care of you?"

The idea of J.D. caring for her would've turned her insides to sweet marshmallow twelve hours ago. Now it made tears prick the backs of her eyes.

Noelle hunched over the clipboard and scribbled her signature while J.D. answered.

"I sure am. What does she need?"

The nurse rattled off a list of instructions, and J.D. peppered her with questions.

Noelle ground her teeth and hardened her heart. *You don't have to pretend anymore.*

Noelle handed the clipboard back to the nurse with her signature on several forms. "I can leave now?"

"Yes, ma'am." She shook her finger in Noelle's face. "You do exactly what this man tells you to do and you'll recover nicely."

"Exactly."

J.D.'s grin had the knuckles of her fist itching to punch him in the gut.

She clenched her jaw instead. "I'm going to get dressed now. Leave."

"I'm expecting the rental-car company to deliver a car to the hospital for me. My truck was totaled. I'll go down and see about that and pick you up outside the main doors of the hospital. Then we'll talk."

"Whatever." She had to get home somehow, and she still had to grill him about Zendaris...and his own identity.

When J.D. and the nurse left the room, Noelle nibbled on the scone and sipped the remaining latte while she got dressed. Applying some lip balm, she inspected herself in the mirror. The crash had given her both a cut and a bump above her right temple. Those wounds were nothing compared to the one J.D. had inflicted on her heart with his deception.

The orderly insisted on wheeling her out of the hospital in a wheelchair, so she sat back and closed her eyes. Maybe this all had a silver lining. If that lying hunk of... hunk knew who was after her, she had a fighting chance.

Maybe not for the relationship she'd been foolishly imagining with J.D., but a chance to confront her stalker head-on. She touched her bandage—maybe not head-on either.

The orderly waited with her on the sidewalk in front of the hospital until J.D. drove up in a rental, a silver SUV.

He and the orderly each took one of her arms and walked her to the passenger side of the vehicle. J.D. helped her up and into the seat, and they both thanked the orderly.

As soon as J.D. hit the driver's seat, Noelle snapped, "Tell me."

"Are you sure you don't want to wait until we get back to the ranch? You might need to be more comfortable than you are now to hear this story."

Her stomach rolled, and she pinned her folded hands between her knees. "Just tell me."

He reached into the backseat and tossed her hat into her lap. "I saved this from the wreckage, along with your bag with your laptop in it."

"Thanks. Now talk."

He adjusted the mirrors and glanced at her. "Nico Zendaris is an international arms dealer."

Her jaw dropped, and she turned to stare at his profile. "You're kidding."

"Would I lie about something like that? Wait, don't answer that."

"He's an arms dealer? Why would an arms dealer be after me? That's insane. I don't believe you."

"You had a roommate in D.C., Abby Warren."

"How do you know about Abby?" A chill crept across her flesh.

"Not from you. Every time I'd ask you a leading question about unusual occurrences lately, you never brought up Abby—not until yesterday. Isn't the sudden disappearance of a roommate unusual? Or does that happen to you all the time?"

She ground her teeth together. "If you knew about Abby, why didn't you just ask me? In fact, why all the lies and deceit?"

"I'll get to my lies and deceit in a minute. Do you want to hear about Abby's lies and deceit first and her connection to Zendaris?"

"Abby has a connection to an international arms dealer?"

"Had. Abby Warren is dead."

Noelle covered her face with her hands. "This is crazy. How? Who? This is too much."

"One thing at a time. Abby's twin sister, Beth, worked for Prospero, an undercover intelligence agency. Through her twin, Abby met a few people, learned a few things and developed a lunatic crush on one of the agents."

She jerked her head up. "You?"

"Not me—my buddy, Cade Stark. Abby was also a computer whiz, but maybe you knew that already."

Cade Stark. Noelle drew her brows together. That name sounded familiar for some reason. "I knew she worked as a private IT consultant. She went after hackers mostly."

"Takes one to know one. She hacked into Stark's computer and nabbed some plans that he had just stolen from Zendaris. To make a long story short, she contacted Zendaris in the end to let him know she had the plans."

"Did he kill her?" Noelle's eye twitched.

"No."

"Did you kill her?" She wanted to know what kind of man she was dealing with—what kind of man she'd been falling for.

"No." He shot her a quick look.

"Where are the plans now?"

"That's the million-dollar question, isn't it, darlin'?"

Widening her eyes, she jabbed a thumb against her chest. "Me? This Zendaris thinks *I* have the plans?"

"Either that or he thinks you know something."

"And so did you."

"What?" It was J.D.'s turn for the look of openmouthed surprise.

"That's why you kept me in the dark all this time. You thought I was in cahoots with Abby or something. You thought I had the plans—maybe you still do."

"You're quick but not completely accurate." His knuckles whitened as he gripped the steering wheel. "I never believed for one minute you had anything to do with Abby's crazy scheme, not after I'd met you."

"Someone did."

He nodded, a quick dip of chin to chest. "Someone whose job it is to be suspicious, but I convinced him otherwise. I told you the truth when I said I was ready to spill everything this morning."

She wedged her boots against the floor of the car. How could she trust him when she didn't even know who he was?

"What's the rest of the story? Who are you, and why are you in Colorado?"

"I thought I'd made that clear. I'm an agent with this intelligence organization—with Prospero."

"You've been watching me? Following me?"

"As soon as we found out about Abby Warren's secret life, we dug into her background and discovered you. We've had our eye on you ever since."

"You probably know more about my life than I do. You obviously knew about my husband's murder." Did he also know Alex had become a control freak, bordering on emotionally abusive?

"I knew about your husband's murder." He covered her hand with his. "Sorry."

If J.D. was sorry, he probably *didn't* know about Alex's obsession with tracking her every movement. She inched her hand away from his warm grasp. Was his name even J.D.?

"What's your name?"

"J.D." He held up two fingers like the Boy Scout he wasn't. "I swear."

"Is that for Jim Davis?"

"Uh, no."

At least he had the decency to blush. "What is your real name? I have a right to know the name of the man who's been following me around for a month."

"Jared Douglas." He held out his hand for a shake.

She ignored it.

"Would I have discovered anything more about Jared Douglas than I did about Jim Davis from a search on the internet?"

"You ran a search on me? Good girl."

Her lips twisted into a snarl. "Don't patronize me. I ran a search on Jim Davis."

He shrugged. "You wouldn't have found much more on Jared Douglas—fewer of us—but it's not like I frequent any social networking sites with my occupation and hobbies listed."

Noelle slumped in her seat and turned her gaze to the landscape, blanketed in freshly fallen snow. She had bigger problems than the identity of her ranch hand turned spy.

She and Abby hadn't been close at all. She'd found her roommate closed off and distant, and that had suited her. The primary requirement she'd had for a roommate after Alex's murder had been neatness—and Abby had fit the bill.

Abby had shared very little of her life. She certainly

didn't tell Noelle where she'd hidden some plans she'd stolen from a dangerous arms dealer.

"No more questions?" J.D. had pulled his rental off the highway and onto the road leading to the ranch.

Should she kick him out now? No. He'd kept her safe the past few days, and she still needed…his protection. Of course, now she knew why he'd been so attentive—he was doing his job. Couldn't let the bad guys get their hands on a prime witness, could he?

"Can't we just tell them?"

"Tell who what?"

"Tell Zendaris and his flunkies that I don't know anything about the plans. They've already searched the apartment in D.C. They've searched my place here. They didn't find anything or they wouldn't have pulled that stunt last night. You'd think they'd just give up and go on to plan B."

The line of J.D.'s jaw hardened as he swung through the gates to the ranch. "Zendaris doesn't give up, Noelle. He wants to question you, and then he'll destroy you."

He threw the SUV into Park and they sat side by side, his words hanging in the air between them.

"Should I leave Buck Ridge?"

"Where would you go?"

"I have some money. I could hide out somewhere, move to a different city."

"And be looking over your shoulder every minute of the day for the rest of your life?"

"What would make Zendaris stop? What would make him leave me alone?"

"A bullet between his eyes."

One look at J.D.'s chiseled profile, and she knew he'd want to be the one to do it. Hugging herself, she said, "I'm sure your agency would've done that by now if they could. Is he that untouchable?"

"He's hard to find, well protected, moves around a lot. We don't have any good pictures of him. We suspect he goes out in disguise most·of the time."

"Seems like you'd have more luck catching a shadow." She drew a tic-tac-toe board in the condensation of the window. "If you can't catch him, how are you going to stop him? When am I ever going to be free of his scrutiny?"

"I know something else that would make him stop harassing you." J.D. yanked the keys from the ignition.

"Besides his death or mine? What? What would stop him?"

"If we got our hands on those plans."

J.D. HELD HIS breath as Noelle dragged her finger through three diagonal *X*'s on her game of tic-tac-toe. "Do you really think I know where they are? I thought you believed me."

"I believe you *think* you don't know where they are."

She shook her head, and her dark ponytail swayed from side to side. "This is getting too confusing for me, and it has nothing to do with the bump on my head. I told you. I have no idea what Abby could've done with those plans. I didn't know of their existence forty-five minutes ago. Heck, I didn't even know Abby well, and it turns out I knew even less about her than I thought I did."

"You lived with her. You at least knew her habits, her hangouts, her moods."

She turned her deep violet-blue eyes on him. "Is this how Zendaris would question me?"

Her barb pricked his conscience. "Trapped in an icy-cold car after just getting released from the hospital? Probably just his style."

Probably much, much worse.

Punching a button, he unlocked the doors of the SUV

and reached in the back for her bag. "Let's get you warmed up inside. I'll get you something hot to drink and another ibuprofen."

"That sounds about right."

This time she stayed in the car until he came around the passenger side and helped her from the vehicle. She clung to his arm when her boots hit the ground.

"Are you okay?"

"A little dizzy."

"I can't imagine why." He'd clobbered her with so much information on the drive back to the ranch, he'd probably induced another concussion.

When they got inside the chilly house, he parked her on the love seat to the right of the fireplace and began stacking cords of wood on the grate. He lit some crumpled newspaper beneath the wood and straightened up, wiping his hands on the seat of his jeans.

"Coffee, tea or…hot chocolate?" The *me* hovered on the tip of his tongue, but he didn't want to push things with her. When she'd discovered his lies, her eyes had flashed fire. She'd softened some when he had explained the situation to her, but her body language still screamed *hands off* when before her ready touch and luscious lips had invited him to explore further.

"Tea is fine." She waved a hand toward the kitchen. "There's a kettle on the stove, and I keep tea bags in the cupboard to the left of the stove."

"I'll find everything. Sit back and relax."

"And start thinking about Abby and her habits?"

"Not right now. Give your brain a rest." He didn't want to elicit any comparisons with Zendaris from her again.

When the kettle whistled, he poured the bubbling water over the tea bag in Noelle's cup, where it turned a light green. He sniffed it and wrinkled his nose—bland and tasteless. He didn't see the point in drinking the stuff even if it was supposed to be good for you.

He returned to the living room, holding the steaming mug in front of him. "How long do you leave the tea bag in?"

"About five minutes. Can you please get me a saucer?"

He grabbed one from the cupboard and paused in the kitchen. "Do you want something to eat?"

She dunked the tea bag into the water several times. "No, thanks. The hospital fed me, and I finished off that scone you brought. Don't you want some tea?"

"No." He tapped the side of his head. "How's the head feeling?"

"It throbs when the ibuprofen wears off, but other than that I'm okay." She sipped the tea through the steam rising from the cup. "What if they had killed us last night? They wouldn't be getting any answers."

"They knew precisely where to run us off the road. It's not like we were going to tumble off the mountain at that spot, and I was driving a big truck. They wanted to shake us up."

"Do you still think they were planning to snatch me from the wreckage?"

J.D. dropped to the floor at her feet. "Not if I had anything to say about it."

She hunched forward, elbows digging into her knees, black ponytail swinging over her shoulder. "Do they know who you are, J.D.? Do they know I'm being protected by a secret agent?"

"Zendaris is aware of our agency. We've foiled his schemes before—in a big way, one that he'll never forget. He knows we stole the plans. Up until a few months ago, he thought we still had them."

"But does he know what you look like? Does he realize you're here in Buck Ridge?"

"I'm not sure." The fire crackled and spit out a shower of sparks. J.D. hitched up to his knees and prodded the logs with a poker. "He probably knows I removed the cameras from your house, but it doesn't take a covert-ops agent to find a few hidden cameras."

"If he has his guys following me, then he has to figure your agency is doing the same thing."

"But he may believe we're doing so at a distance. He knows our agency keeps a low profile."

She tilted her head. "What is Prospero, anyway? Something I would've heard of on the news? Something like the CIA?"

"We're deeper cover than the CIA. You won't hear about us on the evening news or read about our exploits on a website."

Sitting back against the love seat, she curled her legs beneath her and dropped the tea bag onto the saucer he'd placed on the table next to her. "If you can find these plans, what will you do with them? What are they for?"

"I'd rather not tell you."

"You already made that clear, but if you want my help finding those plans, you need to give me something to work with. How will I know what I was supposed to see?" She took another sip of tea, watching him over the rim.

She was good. And she had a point.

Dragging in a breath, he pushed off the floor and perched on the arm of the love seat. "The plans are for an anti-drone, a weapon that can take out our drone missiles, crippling their effectiveness."

"Oh my God. That's big."

"You got that right. That's why it's so important that we

find those plans before Zendaris does. He has the means to build the weapon and then sell it on the open market to any terrorist group or rogue regime that coughs up enough money."

"Where did he get them in the first place? Can't the person who developed those plans just whip up a new set?"

"The person who developed those plans is on our side now. He's not going to be working for Zendaris, or any other weapons dealer or terrorist, anymore."

"Once you find and destroy those plans to keep them out of our enemies' hands, that's it?"

"For now—until the next threat."

"I can help by trying to figure out where Abby stashed the plans." She swirled the tea in her cup, gazing into it as if she could find the answer in some tea leaves. "Are they on paper? Computer disk? Flash drive?"

"The plans weren't on paper, so if they are now, she printed them out. She hacked into my coworker's computer. She could've put the plans on a disk or flash drive. She could've made copies for all we know."

"That could get messy."

"I don't even want to think about that possibility."

Noelle set her cup on the table and rose to her feet. "You've given me a lot to think about. Maybe something will come to me in the shower. I feel hospital-icky."

"Are you sure you feel okay to hit the shower?"

"I'm not dizzy—except from all the info you told me about arms dealers and covert agencies and my unassuming, computer-nerd roommate."

He cupped her elbow. "Do you understand why I had to keep my identity a secret?"

"Sure." She broke away from him and called over her shoulder, "Maybe you should stay here...just in case."

"Of course. I'm not going anywhere."

She slammed the bathroom door on his last syllable.

Sure didn't seem like she understood.

NOELLE STOOD AT the bathroom mirror scraping at the edge of the tape holding her bandage. She tugged the tape from the skin of her forehead and peeled back the bandage. Still snowy-white. At least the bleeding had stopped.

Leaning in closer to the mirror, she traced the stitches with the tip of her finger. The doc said she could let the wound breathe if she felt comfortable without the bandage, but she'd leave it on in the shower to protect her new stitches.

She cranked on the water and shed her clothing, stepping out of her jeans.

How had she gotten mixed up in something like this? Wasn't one traumatic event per lifetime enough? She'd paid her dues. Let someone else have the drama.

The warm water beat between her shoulder blades and streamed down her back. She closed her eyes, replaying scenes in her D.C. apartment with Abby.

Abby hadn't entertained at all. Noelle had met only one of her friends in the almost two years they'd shared space—a quiet, almost shy man who'd picked up Abby for a date.

Abby had spent a lot of time in her bedroom, which she'd turned into an office with a bank of computers against one wall. The police had removed all those computers after she'd disappeared. Maybe that should've clued her in that Abby's disappearance had a sinister aspect to it.

This was the kind of stuff J.D. would want to hear about—Jared Douglas. He'd done a good job making excuses for his lies. How much of what he said and did was faked?

His touches? His kiss?

She turned off the shower without washing her hair, patting the damp bandage in place. Grabbing a towel from the rack, she stepped out of the tub and rubbed a circle in the condensation in the mirror.

Abby's computers… Surely the D.C. police had turned those over to J.D.'s agency. His agency probably ordered the police to remove them. Abby spent a lot of time on her computers.

Her cell phone buzzed against the porcelain, and she snatched it before it vibrated into the toilet.

She swiped the phone against the towel and glanced at the display—a text message from another unknown number. Her heart picked up speed and blood throbbed against her stitches.

Had Ted picked up his new phone?

Her thumb trembled as she hit the button to read the text. She read the words, blinked her eyes and read them again: We have your brother.

Chapter Twelve

Noelle grabbed on to the sides of the vanity and lowered herself to the edge of the tub. She miscalculated and slipped to the floor.

It was a joke. It had to be a joke.

"J.D." She thought she'd whispered his name, but her scream echoed in the small, steamy bathroom.

His footsteps pounded down the hallway, and he threw open the door. "What's wrong? Did you fall?"

He knelt before her, grabbing the towel puddled on the floor and draping it over her naked body.

Her teeth chattered as she held out her phone toward him. "They have Ted."

"What?" He plucked the cell from her hand and brought it close to his face. He cursed and then hugged the towel around her body. "You're shaking. Let's get you out of here. Do you have a bathrobe?"

"They have Ted."

"Maybe they do, maybe they don't, but freezing in the bathroom is not going to help his situation."

She pointed to her pink terry-cloth bathrobe hanging on a hook on the bathroom door.

J.D. stood up, still grasping her phone, and yanked the robe from the hook. He walked back toward her, holding the robe open in front of him. "Can you stand up?"

"I'm okay." She wedged her back against the side of the tub and pushed to her feet. Her knees wobbled as she clutched the towel to her chest.

J.D. folded her robe around her, and she struggled to fit her arms through the sleeves. With his arm around her shoulders, he led her from the bathroom back to the living room, where the fire still crackled. He shoved the love seat around to face the fire and nudged her onto the cushion.

"Do you know how to reach Ted?" J.D. sat beside her and stilled her fidgeting fingers with his hand.

"He was supposed to get a temporary cell phone and call me, but he never did. I didn't even get the names of the people he was crashing with at the Buck Ridge Lodge."

"What about Pierpont? Do you think he saw him up there?"

"I have no idea." She covered her face with her hands. "It's my fault. I should've let him stay here that night."

"If it's anyone's fault it's mine for not warning you sooner. I have one way to solve this." He tossed her phone in the air and caught it. "Text them back."

"R-really?"

"Pretend you don't know what they want. That seems like the safest bet right now. Anyone receiving a message like that would want to know what was happening."

"Y-you want me to contact them?" She drew back from the phone cradled in his palm.

"Do you want to see your brother again?"

She flinched. This was real, just like that gunshot in the gallery. Nodding, she pinched the phone between two fingers as though she were handling a poisonous insect.

"Should I call or text?" She held her breath, waiting for the answer she wanted to hear.

"Do you really want to send texts back and forth with

these people? Do you want them to misconstrue anything you have to say? Call."

That was not the answer she wanted. "What if they don't pick up?"

"Then text, but you need to make the effort. Put yourself in the shoes of someone who knows nothing of the threats against her. Wouldn't you want to call to find out what they want from you?"

She blew out a shaky breath that rattled her frame. They'd broken into her apartment and ranch house. They'd tried to run her off the road. They'd abducted her brother. She wanted to know why. Even though she already knew why.

She pressed the redial button and hunched her shoulders while it rang. Once. Twice.

"Yes?"

The voice had a slight accent—a normal voice. He didn't sound like Darth Vader at all.

J.D. reached over and pressed the speaker button on the side of the phone.

Noelle squeezed her eyes shut and mastered her shallow breath before speaking. "I got your message. What do you want from me? What do you want from my brother? Where is he? Why are you harassing us?"

The man clicked his tongue. "So many questions. We just want to talk, Noelle."

Her name on his lips caused the knots to tighten in her belly. "You have a funny way of initiating a conversation. Why did you break into my apartment in D.C.? It *was* you, wasn't it?"

"We were looking for something."

"No kidding. You trashed my place. Is my brother okay? Can I talk to him?"

"Perhaps. Are the police listening in on this conversation?"

Her gaze shifted to J.D., and he shook his head.

"No. I'm alone."

"That…ranch hand is not with you?"

Again, J.D. shook his head.

"He's in the guesthouse."

"Who is he?"

"My employee and an old friend, and I don't think he's going to stick around much longer, thanks to you. His truck was totaled when you forced us off the road. Why did you do that?"

"I told you, Noelle. We just want to talk to you."

"Well, you're talking to me now. Did you have something to do with my husband's murder? If so, you have to know that I can't identify you. I couldn't give the police anything."

"This has nothing to do with your husband. We want to ask you a few questions about your roommate, Abby Warren."

"Abby?" Her voice squeaked, and J.D. flashed her a thumbs-up.

"Yes."

"Ask away. The police told me she had some…uh… personal issues. I don't know anything more than that."

"Our questioning cannot be done over the telephone. We'd like to meet with you in person."

"Are you kidding? You tried to kill me last night. Why would I want to meet you in person?"

"We had no intention of killing you, Noelle."

"You could've fooled me. Now I want to talk to my brother. And how do I know you even have him? I have no way of contacting him to find out if it's true or not."

"We'll send you a picture of him. And know this, Noelle. If you don't agree to meet with us in person, alone, the consequences could be very grave for your brother."

"Just ask me your damned questions. If you're trying to get some dirt on Abby, I'll tell you everything I know about her situation…over the phone."

"We'll be in touch to set up a meeting." The phone went dead, and Noelle dropped it into her lap.

"You did great." J.D.'s fingers skimmed her cheek.

"Not great enough that he believed me. He still must think I know something. Is that why he's insisting we meet face-to-face?"

"That—and other reasons."

She fisted her hands so that her nails dug into the flesh of her palms. "Will they try to torture the truth out of me?"

"They might shoot you up with truth serum."

"Maybe that's the way to go." She pressed her fists against her stomach. "Let them give me truth serum. I know nothing about those plans."

"But you do. You know they exist, which is another reason why I wanted to keep you in the dark."

"And once they find out I know about the anti-drone plans, even if I don't know their whereabouts, they'll kill me." She grabbed his arm. "Won't they?"

"Noelle."

She flung his arm away from her and jumped from the love seat. Order. She needed order.

She marched to the bookcase and inspected the row of old hardback books from her parents' collection. The titles faced every which way. Some of the books were upside down. Some of the spines were turned inward.

"Noelle, are you okay?"

J.D.'s voice sounded distant, an echo from a million miles away.

She pulled the first book out and put it in the same direction as the next two. She snatched the fourth book and turned it around.

"Noelle?"

J.D.'s warm breath tickled the back of her neck, but the disordered books called to her, demanded her full attention.

The fifth book. The sixth book. *Get in line. Face the same direction.* Her mind gave the commands and her motions followed as if on autopilot. She couldn't stop now even if she wanted to.

And she wanted to.

J.D.'s arms engulfed her from behind, wrapping her in a warm cocoon of safety. But she wasn't safe. She'd never be safe again.

"It's okay, Noelle. I'll make it okay for you."

She spun around, burying her face in his chest. "It's out of control. It's all out of control."

"Shh." He cupped her face, tilting it toward his.

His kisses rained down across her nose, her cheeks, her chin.

She grabbed his flannel shirt, dizzy from his kisses, not her concussion, the books forgotten.

He sifted his fingers through the back of her hair, pulling it loose from the ponytail. After meandering around her face, his lips found their target and his mouth moved over hers, caressing, inviting.

She wanted this. She wanted wild, messy sex. She wanted to shove all the fear and hopelessness of the past few years into a dark corner. She wanted to let go.

She skimmed her hands across J.D.'s unshaven face, the bristles of his beard scratching her palms. When he deepened the kiss, she nipped at his bottom lip.

He murmured against her mouth, "Are you ready? Do you want to do this?"

For an answer, she slid her hands beneath his T-shirt and raked her nails across his back.

The breath hissed between his teeth as he planted his hands on her hips. "Slow down."

But she couldn't slow down. She didn't want to slow down. If she did, she'd have to return to the books. She'd have to move the love seat back to its original location. She'd have to pick up her towel from the bathroom floor and hang it over the rack so the ends lined up evenly.

She pressed the lines of her body along his, her soft curves molding to the sharp planes and hard muscles of his frame. Plowing her fingers through his tangled hair, she pulled his head down for another kiss. This time, she took control, plunging her tongue into his depths, setting the pace of their passion—fast and furious.

He rubbed her arms beneath the sleeves of her robe. "You feel cold. Let's go back to the fire."

He didn't wait for an answer, sweeping her off her feet, cradling her against his chest. He carried her back to the love seat, aptly named, and settled her on a cushion.

When he sat beside her, she crawled into his lap, strad-dling him. Her robe opened beneath her, and the rough denim of J.D.'s jeans chafed her inner thighs.

Tilting his head against the back of the love seat, he measured her with hooded eyes and expelled a ragged breath. "You're killing me here."

The top of her bathrobe gaped open, and she shrugged the terry cloth off her shoulders, slipping her arms from the sleeves. She cupped her breasts and offered them to J.D.

Groaning, he took her right nipple between his lips and sucked it into his mouth.

The pleasure of his touch spiraled right down to her core, and she gasped while undulating against his lap. He thrust his pelvis upward, and she felt the hard outline of his erection.

He switched his attention from her right breast to her left, tracing her aching nipple with the tip of his tongue. He drew back and blew on it, and she arched her back for more.

Sensation. She craved sensation. The senses had to rule over the mind. Had to blot out reasonable thought.

"You're overdressed." She pulled at the buttons on his shirt, her movements so clumsy, he had to finish the job. He tossed the flannel shirt behind him, and then yanked off his T-shirt in one motion.

She drank in the sight of his chiseled chest sprinkled with tawny hair. She brushed her cheek against one perfectly formed pec, his hair tickling her ear. She inhaled his scent—clean and natural. He must've showered at the hotel this morning, and not one for using colognes, he smelled all male.

Alex had always worn that cologne. She'd grown to hate it, and now she hated it even more since one of her attackers seemed to favor it, too.

Stop thinking.

Her fingers crept down his belly and tugged at the button on his fly. Then she moved to the zipper on his jeans, and he cinched her wrist.

"Are you sure about this?"

Spies must have incredible self-control because judging by the bulge in J.D.'s jeans and his erratic breathing he'd have a hard time stopping this train now.

"Why are you asking me that?" She shook off his hands and peeled back his fly. She skimmed her fingernails across the cotton of his briefs.

His entire body shuddered, and he swallowed, his Adam's apple bobbing in his throat. "It's just…" He clenched his jaw as her nails made another pass across his briefs. "You were so upset before. What were you do—?"

She yanked at his waistband and caressed his tight, smooth flesh.

He sighed and repositioned his hips so that she slid off his thighs. Then he pulled his jeans and underwear off together and dragged her back into this lap.

That's right. No thinking allowed. No questions.

She kicked off the robe, still clinging to her lower body, and pressed her inner thighs against his outer thighs. Skin against heated skin, they sizzled when they met.

He ran his hands down her sides, circling her hips. "Do you want to move to the bedroom?"

Shaking her head, she pulled the band from her hair that held the remains of her ponytail. She tilted forward and trailed her hair from J.D.'s chin to his belly.

J.D. reached behind him, grabbed the throw pillow tilted into the corner of the love seat and tossed it to the ground. Then he reclined.

The cushion belongs in the corner.

Noelle clenched her teeth and dug her fingers into J.D.'s shoulders, moving her hips against him.

He cupped her buttocks, the biceps in his arms bunching. "Let's take this onto the floor. We're going to end up falling off this little couch and breaking our necks."

Lifting her against his chest, he slid to the floor. On the way down, Noelle made a grab for her bathrobe, discarded in a tangled heap.

She needed to hang it up.

J.D. rolled on top of her, the firelight picking out the golden highlights in his hair and casting a glow over his bronzed skin. If she couldn't allow herself to let go with this fine specimen of manhood, the crazies really had taken control of her mind.

He dipped his head and ran the tip of his tongue between her breasts.

She rolled her head to the side and caught sight of the edge of the rug, curled under from when J.D. dragged the love seat before the fire.

Her fingers crept toward the wavy rug, and she stared at her hand as if it were some part of her body with a mind of its own. In the confines of her head she screamed, *Stop!*

But the hand wouldn't obey. Slowly, the fingers stretched out and flattened the rug into submission.

"Noelle?" J.D.'s voice rasped in her ear.

"Mmm?"

Is the rug straight enough? Should I try again?

Her fingers walked toward the edge.

"Don't you like that?"

Noelle blinked. "What?"

J.D. pinched her left nipple between calloused fingers while drawing the right between his lips for a soft kiss. The contrast between pain and pleasure drew a garbled cry from her throat as her hips bounced from the floor.

"That's more like it. Thought I lost you." His fingers and his lips switched places and he continued his exquisite torture.

She thrashed her head from side to side as tension coiled in her belly. The fire warmed her face as J.D. warmed her body. A log slipped off the grate and the wood popped.

The log should be on the grate.

The basket holding the logs is too close to the edge and not lined up with the horizontal cement grout between the bricks.

She squeezed her eyes closed and wrapped her legs around J.D.'s hips. "Hurry. Let's go."

J.D.'s body stopped its delicious movements. His fingers, which had been stroking her inner thighs, froze.

Her words had sounded bad.

"I—I want you. I want you inside me. I can't wait."

He rolled from her body, taking all his warmth with him. Sitting up, he rested his forearms on his knees, which he'd drawn up to his chest. "What's wrong?"

"Nothing."

She reached out and rubbed her knuckles along the back of his calf. "Come back to me."

"*You* come back to *me,* Noelle, because you're not into this at all." He dropped his hand and toyed with her fingers. His tone softened. "You're not ready for this. It's my fault. I shouldn't have pushed you. You just found out about your brother. What kind of idiot seduces a woman after she's just found out her brother has been kidnapped?"

"It's not you." She clutched his fingers. "You don't have to be gallant here. You know I jumped your bones. I came on to you—practically ripped off your clothes."

Grinning, he spread his arms wide. "Do you see me complaining?"

She sat up and rubbed the side of her breast against his leg. "We can still do this. I won't rush you. We can spend all afternoon in front of this fire making love."

Her hand hovered over the throw pillow wedged between the love seat and the end table. She curled her hand into a fist, but it was no use. She plucked the pillow from its spot, placed it flat on the floor and began smoothing out the wrinkles in its cover with agitated fingers.

J.D. traced his index finger from the inside of her elbow to her wrist. "What's wrong, Noelle?"

She wanted to deny that there was anything wrong. She wanted to deny the compulsion for order that had crept over her the past few days, ever since she'd returned to the ranch. She wanted to deny that she hadn't made love with a man since the death of Alex.

But J.D. could spot a psycho a mile away.

She punched the pillow and raised her gaze to his, tears flooding her eyes, her nose stinging. "I…I…"

He scooted next to her and wrapped her in a hug, all the sexual content drained from the embrace, despite the fact that they both remained naked, parts of her body still tender and sensitive.

Kissing the side of her head, he tucked her hair behind one ear. "Do you have OCD?"

She shook her head, and a tear crested and dropped onto her cheek. "No—not all the time. I mean, not for a long time and never before—before Alex's murder."

A sob welled in her throat, and she choked it back, but another came on its heels, overwhelming her ability to contain it. Everything the past few days had overwhelmed her ability to contain.

The tears rolled down her face unabated now, the sobs shaking her body.

J.D.'s arms grew tighter around her. Of course he felt sorry for her. Who wouldn't feel sorry for someone whose life was controlled by straightening and organizing and counting and checking?

Her father had felt so sorry for her mother he couldn't leave her—even for someone he really loved.

J.D. pinched her chin, forcing her to look him in the face even though she knew her nose was red and running, her eyes puffy, her lips trembling.

"Why exactly did you think it was a good idea to have wild, hot sex on the living room floor? Not that I minded in the least."

Her bottom lip quivered as she tried to form a coherent response. "I th-thought if I lost myself—" another sob contorted her face "—in—in my senses, I could forget about my compulsions."

He stroked her face, catching her tears on the ends of his thumbs. "Didn't work, huh?"

Shame burned her cheeks as she gazed into his whiskey eyes. She'd used him and he knew it. She'd seduced him, stoked his passion, whipped him up to the point of release—and then denied him.

His chest, still flushed with desire, had just stopped heaving seconds before. His rasping breath had just slowed to a normal pace. She didn't even want to look at the other parts of his body.

"I'm sorry, J.D. What I felt, what I did—I wasn't faking it. I wanted to be with you. I just…"

"You're not ready. Even if you were, this isn't the time or the place."

Her gaze wandered past his body to the nest they'd created before the fire. She couldn't think of a more perfect place.

He snatched the pillow and, crushing it against his crotch, he stood up. He extended a hand to her. "Why don't you lie down and get some rest, and I'll start on some work around this place while we wait to hear from Zendaris's men? I still want to help you out around here."

She pulled her robe into her lap and took his hand. Her nakedness now seemed a sham, and she wrapped her bathrobe around her body and secured the tie.

He must've felt the same because he struggled into his jeans behind the love seat with his back toward her. He said over his shoulder, "Do you need to call someone about your symptoms? Were you seeing a psychiatrist?"

Another wave of shame flooded her body. The humiliation just kept on piling on. "Yes, someone in D.C."

He buttoned his fly and snapped his fingers. "The meds. That's what the meds were for. Will your doctor in D.C.

phone in a prescription for you? Can doctors even prescribe meds across state lines? I'm not even sure."

That's it. He'd relegated her to crazy town.

"I've already done that. A prescription is waiting at the pharmacy, but I don't need medication. This is just a slight—" she circled a hand in the air "—setback."

"Listen." He pulled his T-shirt over his head, and his hair stuck out all over. "I'd characterize getting stalked by a man who instills fear in every drug dealer and terrorist across the globe and then having that man come after your family members more than a setback. You do what you need to do to take care of yourself."

He stuffed his arms in his flannel. "I'm sure you were doing just fine and had been well on your way to recovery, but this is a very special circumstance. Nobody's going to fault you for backsliding under the circumstances—not your doctor, not me."

"But Dr. Eliason can't know the circumstances, can she? She's going to think I failed, that I can't handle everyday pressures."

He strode around the love seat and grabbed her shoulders, giving her a little shake. "Stop that. She's a doctor. She's seen everything. She doesn't make judgments like that. Besides, what do you care if she does? You know the truth. A lesser woman, one who hadn't already had to deal with watching her husband murdered in cold blood, would've fallen apart by now." He loosened his grip and placed a chaste kiss on her forehead. "You're amazing."

Of course he had to say that. And that closed-lipped, dry kiss was probably all she had to look forward to now. Why hadn't she been paying better attention when her nude body had been sprawled beneath his nude body? When his hands had been exploring all her sensitive bits? When his tongue had been teasing her to unbearable passion?

She sighed. "Thanks. I'm going to lie down."

She started for the bedroom, then the buzzing of her phone stopped her. She spun around and almost collided with J.D., reaching for the phone.

"Is it them? Are they calling back with their demands, with news of Ted, with a meeting place?"

She dived for the phone and checked the display, her heart hammering in her chest. "It's another unknown number, a different one."

"Answer it."

She pushed the talk button. "Hello?"

"Hey, Noelle. What's up? I finally got my phone."

Staggering back a step and bumping against J.D.'s chest, she choked out, "Ted?"

Chapter Thirteen

Noelle swayed to the side, and J.D. caught her, lowering her to the nearest chair. Zendaris's guys must be giving Noelle proof of life for Ted. They were allowing him to call to show her he was okay.

Let the bargaining begin.

"Ted, are you okay? What do you mean you got a phone?"

J.D. drew his brows together. They gave Ted a phone? He wiggled his thumb in the air, and Noelle turned on the speaker.

"You're on speaker. J.D. is here. What happened?"

"Why is J.D. always around? Is that guy your shadow or something?"

Noelle turned wide and confused eyes on him.

Hell, he was just as much in the dark as she appeared to be. Why was Ted taking his kidnapping so lightly? Maybe he could get through to him.

"Ted, it's J.D. Are you okay? What did they do to you?"

"Huh? What's the matter with you guys? I know I don't always follow through on my word, Noelle, but is it really such a big deal that I picked up a phone?"

"Ted." Noelle put a hand to her head. "I got a call that you'd been kidnapped."

Ted hooted. "Why would anyone want to kidnap me?

I have nothing, and if they're trying to get to you, I don't think a few hundred grand in life-insurance money is enough to risk a kidnapping. What are you talking about? Is this some kind of joke?"

"It's no joke, Ted. I got a call from some very serious people. They claimed they had you."

Ted laughed.

Did Noelle's brother ever take anything seriously?

J.D. cut across the laughter. "Has anyone approached you? Has anyone been following you?"

"Not unless you count the hot ski bunnies up at the lodge."

Rolling his eyes, J.D. shook his head at Noelle. "Would you even know if someone was following you?"

"Believe me. I've had people on my tail before. I'd notice. What exactly did these guys want in exchange for my worthless life?"

"Never mind." Noelle slumped into the chair. "Just be careful. There's a lot of strange stuff going on in Buck Ridge right now."

"Yeah, well, most of that strange stuff seems to be happening right there at the old homestead—not that it was ever *my* old homestead. Anyway, you have my new number, and I'll let you know if someone tries to kidnap me."

Noelle ended the call and then saved Ted's number in her phone. She tossed the cell onto the coffee table. "What do you think that was all about? Do you think they were bluffing? How could they not know I wouldn't find out? Should I contact them?"

"No. I have no idea what Zendaris is up to, but you do not want to initiate contact this time." J.D. raked a hand through his hair and blew out a breath. He felt as if he'd just been on some giant roller coaster—three times. First, he'd had to back down the sharp peak he'd been climbing making love to Noelle. Then she hit him over the head with the fact that the best damned foreplay he'd experienced in years had been a ploy to squelch her OCD. Now this.

It wasn't like Zendaris to play games—not that the SOB didn't like games.

He massaged his temples. His head ached, along with a few other body parts he'd rather not think about.

"I guess we have to wait and see if Zendaris's men contact you again. Why don't you take that nap? It should be easier now that you know Ted is safe. I'm going to get started on some work."

That's what he needed to unwind this coil in his belly— good, hard manual labor.

"Keep your phone next to you and your shotgun in the corner, even though I'll be right out front on the porch." He patted her back in a brotherly manner. "Are you going to be okay?"

"I'd feel better if I knew what was going on."

"Wouldn't we all?"

AN HOUR LATER, J.D. pulled up the last of the rotted wood from the porch and stood back, hands on hips, surveying the gaps he'd have to cover with plywood.

A truck rumbled down the drive, and J.D. narrowed his eyes, peering at the windshield.

A woman waved out the window and beeped her horn. She parked the truck next to Noelle's and hopped to the ground. Long, dark hair streamed from a knit cap on her head, and she raised a gloved hand in greeting.

"Is Noelle around?"

"She's home, but she's resting." J.D. leaned on the handle of the pickax.

The woman flipped back her hair and strode toward the ripped-up porch. "And you are?"

His muscles tensed and his nostrils flared, picking up the woman's musky perfume. "I'm helping out Noelle around the ranch."

"I can see that." She fluttered gloved fingers at the pile of rotted wood. "I'm Tara Nettles from down the road. I grew up with Noelle…and Ted."

Noelle had mentioned her friend Tara before. She'd been involved with Ted. Too bad Ted had moved on to those hot ski bunnies, although this woman, with her flowing dark hair and doe eyes, fit that description as well. She and Noelle could be sisters.

Bracing the pickax against the porch railing, J.D. held out his hand. "Good to meet you."

She clasped his ungloved hand in a strong grip, sizing him up with her dark eyes—pretty in their own right, but they couldn't compare to Noelle's deep violet-blue eyes.

"Noelle didn't mention that she was in the market for a handyman. I could've recommended a few locals."

J.D. shrugged. "We sort of ran into each other, and it just worked out."

"Were you the one driving the truck that crashed last night? I heard Noelle spent the night in the hospital. That's why I'm here."

"She got a concussion and a cut on the head. She's fine, but she needs her rest."

"That girl doesn't need any more traumas in her life." Tara placed her hands on her hips and planted her booted feet about a foot apart. "So I hope you're not the type of man to roll in dragging a wagonload of drama with you."

She had no idea who had all the drama following her.

"Me?" He crossed his arms and grabbed his biceps, feeling the chill now that he'd stopped working, or maybe it was just the icicles shooting from this woman's eyes. "Drama-free."

Tara snorted. She actually snorted.

"Yeah, right. You look about as dangerous as they come, cowboy." She shook her finger at him. "Don't toy with Noelle's emotions."

She *really* had no idea.

He could give her an earful about how Noelle had just led him down a heated path of seduction, only to cut him off cold. Technically, he'd been the one to call it quits but when she'd told him to hurry up and get it over with that had pretty much punctured his balloon.

He held up his hands. "I'm here to work."

And to do his job protecting Noelle.

"Keep it that way." She'd started to spin on her boot heels when the front door opened.

"Tara?"

Tara peered around J.D. "Are you all right, Noelle? Mom and I heard about the crash."

"I'm okay." Noelle, still in her bathrobe, her hair even more tousled than before, took a tentative step onto the porch.

"Careful!" J.D. sprang onto a slab of solid wood. "I ripped out the rotting wood, and there's not a whole heckuva lot left to the porch. You shouldn't be out in the cold anyway with just a robe on."

He curled an arm around Noelle's waist and nudged her back into the house. When he glanced back at Tara, her dark eyes had gotten even frostier as her gaze bounced between him and Noelle.

"Is it okay if I come in for a visit, Noelle, or are you still…resting?"

"Come on in. I'll make us some tea." She glanced at the sky. "Or something stronger if it's not too early for you."

"Tea is fine. Even though it's five o'clock somewhere, in Buck Ridge it's still only two."

"Is that all? It felt like I'd been asleep for hours."

"How's your head?" J.D.'s fingers itched to smooth the hair back from her bandage and lay a kiss on its edge. But he needed to back off now that he realized he'd been all wrong in reading Noelle's signals. Not to mention the penetrating stare emanating from Tara.

How had he ever characterized those as doe eyes? Tara had wolf eyes, and she was sizing him up as prey.

She planted a boot against the first step. "Is this safe?"

J.D. hopped back down the porch to help Tara across, and then handed her into the house next to Noelle. "Let Tara make the tea, Noelle. You still need to take it easy."

Tara turned, her arms spanning the doorway as she wedged her hands against the doorframe. "I've got this, cowboy."

He saluted. No wonder Ted had hightailed it out of here.

"WHERE DID YOU find *him?*" Tara grabbed her by the shoulders and spun her around, her fingers kneading the terry cloth. "And are you naked under here? Why are you running around naked under your bathrobe with that—" she waved her hand at the front door "—hunk working outside?"

"Take a breath." Noelle crossed index finger over index finger and held them up in Tara's face. "He's out there. I'm in here. I think I have a right to wear anything I damn well please under my robe—including nothing."

"You slept with him." Tara skipped around the room. "I can't believe it. You slept with him—a stranger. When you go, you go big—and hot!"

"Calm down." Noelle wandered into the kitchen and filled the kettle. "I did *not* sleep with J.D."

Came damn near close to it before her ridiculous OCD tendencies got the better of her. Now she'd lost her chance.

She could tell by the way he'd awkwardly patted her back before he'd sent her to the bedroom alone to take a nap. And the way he backed up when she faced him when before the electricity sizzling between them had drawn them close.

Tara bustled into the kitchen, shooing with her hands. "You heard the man. I'll take care of the tea. You sit down."

With the kettle on the stove, Tara returned to the living room and hung over the back of the love seat. "So where did you meet him?"

Noelle curled her toes into the carpet before the fireplace, where she and J.D. had been in each other's arms just a few hours ago.

"He helped me out with the truck and one thing led to another." She crossed her legs beneath her. "Why are you so giddy, anyway? The way you were looking at him outside, I thought you were going to grab the shotgun out of your truck and run him off my property."

"Just wanted to warn him that someone around here has your back. But as long as he's a good guy, I say go for it."

"Go for what? He's helping me out around the ranch." Noelle folded her hands in her lap. *And helping me ward off an international arms dealer who thinks I have something I don't.*

"If you say so."

The kettle whistled, and Tara turned and made for the kitchen. She called over her shoulder, "It's been two years since Alex died, and I don't think you've had a date since, have you?"

"Not exactly." Did rolling around on the floor naked with J.D. count as a date?

Tara floated from the kitchen, balancing two cups on two saucers. She set them both down on the table, the ends of the tea bags fluttering with the movement.

"I think it's time you give it a shot. You've laid all your…issues to rest, and you deserve some happiness."

Noelle's gaze darted to the edge of the rug she'd smoothed out while J.D. had been worshipping her body with his tongue and touch. "I don't know. Some of the old issues are still hanging around."

"It's to be expected." Tara slurped her tea. "Your husband was shot in front of you, and then his killer turned the gun on you. Who wouldn't have problems with that? But your issues are not deal breakers when it comes to dating—a little anxiety and—" she waved a hand in the air "—that other stuff."

The incident in the gallery hadn't gone down quite like that, but who had to know?

Noelle took a deep breath. "That other stuff is called OCD, and it could definitely be a dating deal breaker."

Hadn't it just broken the deal with J.D.?

"Pfft. If you run into some guy who can't handle that, he's not worth dating anyway. In fact, that's a great way to separate the jerks from the good guys."

Noelle blew on her tea, creating little ripples in the light green liquid. "For someone obsessed with the good guys, you sure spent a lot of time trying to make it work with Ted—not such a good guy."

"Ouch. What a way to turn the subject on me."

"Have you seen him since he's been back?"

"I saw him at the Buck Ridge Lodge last night. Must've been just about the time J.D. was crashing his truck. He was with that friend of yours, Bruce Something the Third, who said he'd just had dinner with you and your handyman."

"Oh, is that why you thought we were dating?"

"Why else would you bring the hired help along to dinner with a friend?"

"You met the friend."

"He wasn't so bad—good-looking guy."

"Bruce must've told you he was a third because I don't think Ted would've introduced him like that."

"Ted didn't introduce him at all. Bruce took over to make up for your brother's spotty etiquette."

"Bruce Pierpont the Third isn't my type, but you might like him."

"He's rich, isn't he?"

"Loaded."

"That's my new type."

The front door swung open, and J.D. stuck his head inside the house. "Is it safe?"

Tara hopped up from the love seat. "Why wouldn't it be?"

"Just want to make sure I'm not intruding."

Noelle said, "You sure were making a lot of noise out there. Did you finish?"

"Finished tearing out the wood, and I nailed some plywood over the gaps. It's safe to walk on now."

"If you do good work, maybe my mom and I can hire you to do some jobs around our ranch. Speaking of Mom, I have to get going, Noelle. I have to pick her up from town, along with a few prescriptions. I dropped Mom off to have lunch with Mrs. Corcoran."

"Do you think you can pick up a prescription for me?" She glanced at J.D. "No hurry. I'm not currently taking the meds now, but it's good to have them around."

"No problem. I'll pick it up for you."

"I'll walk you out."

"And I'll make sure you get across that porch safely." J.D. pushed the front door wider and stepped back outside.

Tara gave her a quick hug. "Take care of that head. I'm

so glad you came out of that okay. You can come and pick up the prescription from me later."

"Will do. Thanks for dropping by." Noelle stood on the threshold as J.D. took Tara's arm and guided her down the porch. He'd just scored some more points in Tara's good-guy tally.

Tara waved before ducking into her truck, and J.D. joined Noelle at the door.

"She's the suspicious type, isn't she?"

"Just protective."

"That's a good thing."

The engine of Tara's truck cranked once and sputtered out. She gave it another try. It revved but never turned over.

"Uh-oh. What is it with you ladies and your trucks?"

J.D. jogged toward the truck. Still in her robe and fuzzy slippers, Noelle stayed put.

He stuck his head under the hood and called out instructions to Tara, but the truck wouldn't start. Guess he couldn't fix everything.

Tara stomped across the yard back to the porch. "Can you believe this? I just had Zach work on this piece of junk last month. I hate to ask you, Noelle, but I really have to pick up my mom. Can I borrow your truck? I can bring it back tonight when I get Mom home. I still have the other truck and Zach can give me a ride back when he tows this heap."

"No problem. Keep it for as long as you like. J.D. can chauffeur me around in his rental." She lifted a brow in his direction, and he nodded.

Noelle slipped back inside the house and grabbed the extra set of keys to the truck. She tossed them to Tara.

"Thanks. You're a lifesaver." Tara jingled the keys in the air.

When she drove out of the front gate, Noelle turned to

go back inside the house, stopping midway. "Are you ready to take a break? Do you want something to drink or eat? You never had any lunch."

"I did have dessert."

She'd been out of the flirting game so long, it took her several seconds to catch his meaning. Warmth flooded her cheeks, and she gurgled some inane response.

J.D. held up his gloved hand. "Sorry. Lame joke."

Is that what he thought of her lovemaking efforts? Her spine stiffened, and she turned her back on him. "So, something to eat?"

"I could use something, but I'll get it myself if you don't mind me clattering around your kitchen. Do you have any of those bagels left?"

"I do. Help yourself. I'm going to get dressed."

She closed the door to her bedroom and yanked open her lingerie drawer. It was about time she put on some underwear. She didn't expect a repeat performance from J.D. He wasn't the type of man to be used twice, and if she were completely honest with herself, that's what she'd been doing.

Not that she hadn't enjoyed being with him when her mind was present and in the moment. *Enjoy?* That word didn't begin to describe the feelings he'd aroused in her.

She shook out a pair of jeans and stepped into them, stuffing her feet back into her fuzzy slippers. Just because she was getting dressed didn't mean she had to leave the house.

"Noelle?" J.D. tapped on the bedroom door.

She grabbed the sweater she'd laid out on the bed and pulled it over her head, giving J.D. a muffled response. "Yeah?"

"It's your phone. I checked the display. Ted's calling."

Her heart thumped a little harder as she folded down the collar of her turtleneck. "Answer it before he hangs up."

As she scuffed to the door, she heard J.D.'s voice.

"Yeah. She's right here."

She threw open the bedroom door and held out her hand for the phone. She couldn't help the slight tremor in her fingers, but if he was the one calling he must be okay.

She swallowed and put a smile in her voice. "What's up, Ted?"

"It's Bruce."

Shaking her head at J.D., she lifted her shoulders. "What about Bruce?"

"He's had an accident, Noelle."

A zigzag of fear ran up Noelle's back, and she automatically pushed the speaker button so J.D. could hear the conversation. This couldn't be a coincidence.

"What kind of accident, Ted? Is he okay?"

"Noelle, he—he's dead."

Chapter Fourteen

Noelle reached out with her hand. J.D. didn't know if she sought balance or comfort, but he offered both by pulling her close against his side.

A tremor rolled through her body, and J.D. tightened his grip around her waist. He shouted into the phone, adrenaline amplifying his voice. "What happened?"

"It was a skiing accident. Bruce was heading down a triple-black-diamond run, took a wrong turn and skied off a cliff."

Noelle licked her lips. "Triple black diamond? Bruce was a good skier, but he was cautious. There's no way he would've attempted one of the most difficult runs on the mountain."

"He must've been feeling confident because he attempted it—and failed."

J.D. cut in. "When did this happen?"

"Just a few hours ago. I'd heard about an accident on the mountain, but I didn't know it was Bruce until later. Sheriff Greavy wants to talk to you, Noelle. I told him Pierpont was here visiting you."

J.D. took the phone that Noelle held between them with a trembling hand and clamped it to his ear. "Was Pierpont with anyone? Were there any witnesses to the accident?"

Noelle's body jolted against his. She knew as well as

he did that Pierpont's accident was related in some way to Zendaris. But what did Zendaris's men hope to gain from killing Noelle's friend? Had they questioned him first?

"As far as I know, Pierpont was on his own. Maybe if he'd been with others, they could've talked him out of taking that run."

"Have they recovered the body?"

Noelle sobbed against his chest and he stroked her hair. She needed him now even if she had played him for a fool.

"Yeah, search and rescue brought him down."

"Do you know if foul play is suspected?"

"Foul play? You mean like murder? Why would…?" Ted stopped and sucked in a noisy breath. "What's going on? First, you two give me the third degree about people following and kidnapping me and now this. Does Bruce's accident have something to do with that crank call Noelle got about me?"

"It just might. If you happen to see Greavy, tell him I'm on my way."

"Is this connected to Alex's murder? Is someone after Noelle?"

"We're not sure. But, Ted?"

"Yeah?"

"Don't go down any triple-black-diamond runs."

J.D. ended the call and eased Noelle into a chair.

Rocking forward, she covered her face with her hands. "This is my fault. This is all my fault."

She already blamed herself for her husband's death. J.D. wasn't going to allow her to take responsibility for this one, too.

"Stop." He knelt in front of her and grasped her wrists, pulling her hands away from her wet face. "Put the blame where it belongs—on Zendaris and his thugs."

She sniffled, her gaze locking onto his. "They thought Bruce was my brother, didn't they? That must be it."

Her fear hadn't clouded her reasoning skills, as the same thought had been forming in his mind as well. "That's a possibility. It explains the phone call. They thought they had Ted. They must've discovered soon after talking to you that they had the wrong guy."

"That's why they never called me back with their demands." She wriggled a wrist free from his grip and rubbed the back of her hand across her nose. "They were too busy getting rid of Bruce. Why didn't they just let him go?"

Sitting back on his heels, he released her other wrist. "You know the answer to that. They don't leave loose ends, especially a loose end like Pierpont with his connections. I'm sure he stupidly informed them who he was. Maybe he even thought he and his family's millions were the intended target."

"Which is why they're going to kill me whether or not they get any answers from me about Abby."

"Not if I stop them first."

"How are we going to do that? They haven't shown their faces yet. We have a vague description of the truck that ran us off the road last night, but you know they've ditched that by now."

"They'll make a mistake. Hell, they already made a mistake. They grabbed the wrong guy. They're getting desperate."

"The only reason they haven't nabbed me yet is because of you, isn't it? They would've plucked me off the street by now, or maybe even from my own house, if you hadn't been on the scene."

He placed his hands on the cushion of the chair on either side of her thighs and leaned in, almost touching her nose with his. "That's why I'm here. Do you think Prospero was going to allow Zendaris to get his hands on Abby Warren's roommate?"

She blinked and her long, dark lashes shimmered with unshed tears. "*Propsero* had to make sure I wasn't in league with my roommate first."

"Can't be too careful." He huffed out a breath, stirring the ends of her hair, and then pushed to his feet.

At least he'd made it clear that he was acting as her protector in the name of Prospero and not because he had some special feeling for her. Not that at all.

"I'm going to see Sheriff Greavy and find out if he can shed any more light on Pierpont's accident than Ted did. Maybe someone saw Pierpont with someone on the slopes. Maybe there's camera footage somewhere that will help us ID these guys."

"I'm coming with you."

"Are you feeling up to it? I don't want to leave you here by yourself, but I also don't want you pushing yourself."

"I'm fine. I don't even have a headache anymore."

He brushed at the dirt on his jeans. "I'm going to shower first and change clothes."

"Do it here."

She didn't have to tell him twice. And if she didn't ask him to move in here, he'd have to propose it himself.

"I dropped my bag in the guesthouse when you were sleeping. I'm going to run over and grab some clothes."

She stood, framed by the door, watching him while he jogged to the guesthouse. He grabbed a duffel bag full of clothes he hadn't unpacked yet. Hell, he'd take the whole thing over. He slung the bag over his shoulder as he walked through her door, and she didn't blink an eye.

After his shower, he dressed in the steam of the bathroom and slicked back his hair. Wiping the condensation from the mirror with his fist, he leaned in close and rubbed his knuckles across his stubble. He could use a shave, but he wanted to catch the sheriff before nightfall.

He might have to tell Greavy everything later, or at least as much as Prospero would allow.

Pushing open the bathroom door, he stepped into the hallway, dragging his bag after him.

"Ready?" Noelle peered down the hallway. A pair of snow boots had replaced the fuzzy slippers and she'd pulled the white gauze from her wound, going with a bandage in its place.

"Yep." He held up the duffel bag by the strap.

"You can put that in my bedroom...for now."

He crossed the hall and dropped the bag by the door just inside her room. It didn't mean a thing.

She grabbed both of their jackets from the hooks by the front door and tossed his to him. "At least it stopped snowing."

She swung open the front door, and J.D. welcomed the blast of cold air that assaulted his face. He had no idea how he was going to be able to spend the night in Noelle's house with her soft, warm body under the same roof.

Maybe he'd have to sleep with the windows open.

He unlocked the rental SUV and helped Noelle inside. "Have you heard from Tara? Is she getting her truck towed?"

"I haven't heard from her yet, but that's not unusual. Once her mother and Mrs. Corcoran get to talking, there's no stopping them. Poor Tara's probably stuck listening to their gossip."

"They're going to have a lot of gossip to go over now."

"I can't believe Bruce is gone. It seems every time..." She clamped her bottom lip between her teeth.

He raised a brow in her direction, waiting for her to finish, but she pressed her nose to the window instead.

"Do you think Bruce's killers made a connection between me and Bruce? I'm thinking they didn't once they found out he wasn't my brother. Otherwise, they would've just substituted him for Ted as a hostage."

"Better for them to have a brother than a friend as a hostage, but you might be right." J.D. adjusted the rearview mirror and gave it a glance. "That means they weren't around the lodge during our dinner with Bruce or they would've seen us with him."

"So how did they mistake him for Ted? They look nothing alike."

Hunching his shoulders, J.D. braced his hands against the steering wheel. "Maybe they saw Ted and Bruce together that night we had dinner and got their wires crossed. Tara told us she'd seen Ted with Bruce that night. I do know Zendaris can't be happy about the screwup. He does not tolerate incompetence from his henchmen."

Noelle zipped up her jacket even though he'd cranked on the heat as soon as he started the car. "Then he's probably not a very happy arms dealer right now because whoever's after me has messed up a few times."

"And they'll continue to mess up because they're not getting anywhere near you." His words rang with confidence. He knew he'd lay down his life to protect this woman.

"I wish I could figure out where Abby hid those plans. If we could find the plans, Zendaris's game would be over. He'd have no reason to keep hunting me down."

"I haven't wanted to pressure you, Noelle, but anything you could remember would help us out. It would've been about four months ago, right before she disappeared from your life."

"That's when she stole the plans from the Prospero agent?"

"Yeah. What was going on with her? Did she travel any-where? Open any new accounts with safe-deposit boxes? Dig any holes under the carpet?"

Noelle drew her brows together and toyed with the gloves in her lap.

"That last one was a joke." J.D. nudged her with his elbow, not that he expected her to be laughing.

"If only she *had* dug a hole under the carpet." She drummed her fingers on the dashboard. "Abby did have some computer problems around that time."

"Too bad she didn't have computer problems before she hacked into Cade's computer to lift the plans."

"J.D." Her fingers stopped their nervous tapping, and her nails slid from the dashboard.

"Did you remember something?" His pulse thudded in his temples while he waited for her response.

"Abby had to use my computer."

His blood raced through his veins, and he had to practi-cally gasp for breath. "Abby Warren was using your com-puter? For what?"

"To access her emails and client sites and—" She pressed three fingers to her lips. "You don't think she put something on my computer, do you?"

"Did you notice anything different about your computer after she used it? Additional files?"

"No, but then, I don't know what half the files on my computer do, anyway. I wouldn't notice anything differ-ent." She snapped her fingers. "Except…"

J.D. had to grind his teeth to keep his head from ex-ploding. This had to be it. Abby put the plans on Noelle's computer. But why hadn't Zendaris's men stolen the com-puter? The D.C. police had removed all of Abby's com-puters on Prospero's orders, but nobody had thought to check Noelle's.

Where *was* Noelle's computer right now? He'd rescued it from his truck after the crash, so she had to have it here somewhere.

"Except what, Noelle?"

She'd twisted her fingers into knots, her puzzled gaze boring into the road outside the window.

"Sh-she did some stuff on my computer for security purposes, she said at the time."

"What kind of stuff?"

"She added some passwords and security measures to some of my folders. She warned me that any good hacker could get into my computer and compromise my data, even steal my identity."

J.D. snorted. "That's the pot calling the kettle black."

"Here." Noelle tapped on the window. "The sheriff's substation is in this direction."

J.D. took the turn, but this conversation interested him much more than what Sheriff Greavy could tell them about Pierpont's death.

"So, she had you add some passwords to your folders. Is that all?"

"Yeah, but she could've been doing anything on my computer."

"Which is where?"

"Huh?"

"Where is your computer? I haven't seen it yet since I pulled it from the wreckage."

"It's either at the house or in the truck. I can't remember if I took it out of the truck."

"I'm wondering why Zendaris didn't go for your laptop the first time he broke into your place in D.C."

"It wasn't there. I take it with me to work, and that's when they broke in."

"And when they broke into the ranch house?"

"I had it with me in the truck."

"So as far as Zendaris's men know, you don't have a computer, or since it wasn't staring them in the face when they broke into first your apartment and then your house, it didn't occur to them to look for one." Just like it hadn't occurred to him.

He parked the car in front of the substation, and Noelle unsnapped her seat belt. "This is all supposition. Why would Abby put those plans on my computer? Anything could've happened to them from there. My computer could've crashed and she would've lost everything."

"But she made sure that wasn't going to happen. Those security measures she put into play on your laptop must've covered the file she put on your hard drive. That woman knew her way around a motherboard. We could've used her on Prospero. Too bad she was crazy."

Noelle's lips tightened as she got out of the car. She slammed the door behind her.

J.D. jumped in his seat as the car rocked with the force of the slam. Whoa! Did he just hit a nerve? Did Noelle believe he thought she was crazy for that OCD stuff?

He'd have to set her straight on that. If the only thing she manifested after all she'd been through the past few years was a little obsessive-compulsive behavior, he'd nominate her for the superhero hall of fame.

But first they needed to check that computer.

The cramped sheriff's substation on the mountain buzzed with activity—it was not every day a billionaire entrepreneur skied off the side of a mountain. Even a few members of the press hung on the fringes, ready for a statement or a piece of information that could spice up their stories.

If they only knew.

Zendaris would find out soon enough that his guys

had committed an even bigger screwup than snatching the wrong man. The man they'd snatched happened to have a public profile, and his death would generate some publicity. Zendaris hated publicity.

J.D. draped an arm around Noelle's shoulders and guided her toward the sheriff's closed office door. J.D. tapped on the glass.

An officer peeked through the crack in the door. His scowl dissolved when his gaze fell on Noelle. "Ms. Dupree, Sheriff Greavy is expecting you."

J.D. squeezed into the room beside Noelle just in case there was some question as to whether or not the sheriff was expecting him, too.

Sheriff Greavy looked up from his computer screen and tipped his glasses to the end of his nose. "Jarvis, try to clear the room out there. Have a seat, you two."

When Jarvis had shut the door behind him, Greavy hunched over his desk. "Bruce Chandler Pierpont the Third was in Buck Ridge to visit you, Noelle?"

"He was here to ski, knew I lived in the area and dropped by. I wouldn't say his sole purpose for coming to Buck Ridge was to visit me."

"You ruled him out as your stalker?"

She tucked an errant strand of dark hair beneath her knit cap. "Not necessarily, but I have no proof that he was the one stalking me."

J.D. trained his gaze on Sheriff Greavy's grizzled face so that he wouldn't give away his surprise at Noelle's answer. Guess she didn't want to involve the local P.D.

"You didn't confront him about it?"

"No. We all had a pleasant dinner last night—that's it. We discussed some plans we'd had previously for turning my guesthouse into an art studio and just sort of left things hanging."

"Why all the questions, Sheriff? Pierpont's death was a skiing accident, wasn't it?"

The sheriff tapped his chin with his pen. "As far as we can tell."

"Do you have reason to suspect foul play, Sheriff? Was Pierpont alone when he went over? Were there any witnesses?"

Sheriff Greavy's shaggy gray brows collided over his nose as his gaze sharpened on J.D. Then he slumped back in his chair. "He was alone. No witnesses to the actual accident. There were several people on the run with him, but they were all going too fast to see anything. Folks behind him just saw him take a turn and disappear between the trees."

"Do the lift operators remember anything? Was there anyone with him on the lift?"

"We questioned them." Greavy spread his hands. "Nothing unusual. I wanted to find out if Noelle could shed any light on Pierpont's life, especially considering that camera in your house appeared just about the time Pierpont showed up."

"Yeah, I had thought about that, too." Noelle leaned forward and dug her elbows into Greavy's desk. "But I didn't ask, and Bruce didn't tell."

The sheriff steepled his fingers as if in prayer. "Could he have been suicidal? Going off that cliff is an act of a very bad skier who had no business on that run or someone who was suicidal."

Or someone who was forced off by a man holding a gun to his back.

Zendaris's men would've wanted Pierpont's death to look like an accident.

"I can't imagine Bruce being suicidal." Noelle turned to J.D. "Did he seem despondent to you over dinner?"

"I didn't know the guy, but if that's his despondent I'd be blown away by his happy."

"We already notified the family, and I have a feeling Bruce Chandler Pierpont the Second is going to send an army of his own private investigators out here to look into things." Greavy heaved a heavy sigh. "That type is never satisfied with the job we do."

Noelle convulsively kicked J.D.'s foot under the table. If Bruce's father started nosing around, he could get into a lot of trouble. "Let me know if you need anything else from me, Sheriff Greavy. I'm not going anywhere."

Sheriff Greavy stood up and said, "Will do, Noelle. How's your head?"

She touched the bandage. "It's fine—just a mild concussion."

"You should've been driving instead of your friend here. You know these roads like the back of your hand."

"I don't know if I could've avoided that accident either. We hit a patch of ice. You know how that goes."

"Yep." He gave Noelle the same stare he'd turned on him a few minutes ago. "With everything that's gone on since you've been back, including your friend's death, you must be ready to hightail it back to D.C."

"It's been an…eventful few days, but I still have some business to attend to in Buck Ridge."

"Hope that still includes sprucing up your ranch." Greavy's eyes flicked to J.D.

Before Noelle could respond, a clamor of voices arose from the room outside the sheriff's door.

J.D.'s pulse ticked up. Had they discovered something about Pierpont's accident? Witnesses? Suspects?

He jumped from his seat with Noelle hot on his heels, but neither of them could beat Sheriff Greavy to the door.

He flung it open while muttering, "What the hell is going on out there?"

A hysterical woman held court in the middle of the substation, waving her arms and screeching unintelligible words. She jerked her head up. Black hair whipped across a tear-mottled face.

Noelle stiffened beside him as his own gut rolled.

What was a visibly upset Tara doing at the sheriff's substation?

"Noelle!" Tara clawed her way through the small clutch of officers and threw herself into Noelle's arms.

Noelle soothed her friend, smoothing a hand over her tangled hair, while her gaze skewered J.D. "What happened? What's wrong?"

Tara sobbed against her shoulder and then pulled away. "I was carjacked or hijacked or something."

Noelle gripped Tara's shoulders. "Someone stole my truck?"

J.D. cursed under his breath—not that anyone could hear him since Tara decided to let loose with another wail.

"No. I have your truck here."

J.D. wiped a hand across his mouth, where his upper lip sported beads of sweat. So she still had the truck and she seemed safe. Had something happened to her mother?

"What happened, Tara? Are you okay?" Noelle drew her in for another hug.

Tara continued in a muffled voice, "I dropped Mom off and decided to save you a trip and drop off the truck and your prescription and to see if J.D. could give me a ride back to my ranch, but you weren't home. I called Ted to see if he knew where you'd gone, and he told me you were up here talking to Sheriff Greavy."

An officer handed Tara a box of tissues.

She grabbed a handful and mopped her face, then took

a shuddering breath. "When I got back into the truck, two men came at me."

"Oh my God. Did they hurt you?"

J.D. moved behind Noelle to see Tara's face. Had Zendaris's men believed they had Noelle? Another case of mistaken identity?

"They roughed me up." She looked down at her jacketed arm, where the men had probably grabbed her. "And they had a gun."

Sheriff Greavy had been listening to Tara's story, hanging back by the door to his office, but he stepped forward when she mentioned the gun.

"Hold on, Tara. A couple of men held you up with a gun? Do you have a description? What did they take?" His gaze skipped to the purse slung over her shoulder.

"They were wearing ski masks and dark jackets. They could've been anyone." Her eyes darted around the room; the officers had gotten back to business.

"Vehicle?" Greavy crossed his arms.

"It must've been parked on the road because I sure as hell didn't see any car drive onto Noelle's property. They came at me on foot and then made me lie on the ground when they took off." She brushed at her snow pants as if just remembering she'd been lying on the ground.

J.D. put a hand on Noelle's back. Zendaris's men had been on her ranch again. He should've put cameras up before fixing the porch.

Greavy cleared his throat. "Two men accosted you with a gun at your truck, um, Noelle's truck, at gunpoint. They didn't harm you, and they didn't steal the truck. Then they made you lie on the ground while they took off. I guess I'm missing something here. What did they take?"

Tara blew her nose. "I'm so sorry, Noelle."

Noelle took a step back from Tara, leaning against J.D.'s chest. "What? Why?"

The air felt heavy, and J.D. held his breath.

"Noelle, they stole your laptop."

Chapter Fifteen

Noelle stumbled back farther, and J.D. held her against his solid chest. When hadn't he been there for her in the past few days?

A selfish thought skimmed across her mind—*now they'll leave me alone.* She didn't allow that thought to take root. As crazy as it sounded to her, the theft of her laptop had serious consequences for her country. This transcended her petty issues and even her safety.

If the plans were even on the laptop. She and J.D. didn't know for sure and neither did Zendaris.

"I'm so sorry, Noelle. I know you kept a lot of ideas for your art on there." Now in the role of comforter, Tara sniffled and patted Noelle's arm. "I-is there any chance you have one of those backup services?"

J.D. tightened his grip on her shoulders, but Noelle had to disappoint him. That would've solved their problem if they could've retrieved those plans from a backup server. Is that why Abby hadn't recommended one along with all her other security recommendations?

"I don't have one of those services. But don't worry, Tara." She straightened the back that might no longer have a target on it. "I backed up a lot of my work on flash drives and CDs. The important thing is that you're unharmed."

"The important thing is to nail these thieves." Sheriff Greavy jerked his thumb toward the open door of his office. "I want a statement from you, Tara, from the beginning. I'm not going to tolerate masked men roaming through Buck Ridge committing armed robbery."

Noelle squeezed Tara's hand. "Go ahead. We'll wait for you at the lodge, and I'll give you a ride back in the truck to your place. Did Zach ever come out to my ranch to tow your truck?"

"Yeah, he did. Too bad he wasn't still there when I returned. Those clowns never would've tried that stunt if Zach had been there."

Noelle gave her a tight smile. If Zach had been there at the same time as the *clowns,* he'd be dead.

J.D. followed her out of the sheriff's substation and into the frigid air. The pale yellow sun had already disappeared behind the mountains, leaving a biting cold to take over the night.

Their boots crunched the snow in unison, the only sound between them, as they walked toward the Buck Ridge Lodge. The bright lights and warmth of the lobby had them shedding their jackets as soon as they walked through the door.

Chatty skiers and boarders looking for some warmth and atmosphere clustered around the fireplace, so J.D. steered her toward a couple of armchairs in the corner.

Noelle tossed her jacket over the back of the chair and swept the hat from her head before collapsing against the soft cushions. Extending her legs in front of her, she tapped her boots together. "If Abby put those plans on my laptop, Zendaris has them now."

"How did he know to go after the computer?"

"You're asking me?" She spun her cap around one hand. "They probably saw your rental missing from the ranch and when they saw Tara pull up in my truck, they figured they hit pay dirt."

"You think they mistook her for you?"

"Makes sense. We look similar, unlike Bruce and Ted. By the time they realized their error, they'd spotted the laptop, some lightbulbs went off in their heads and they grabbed it."

"I hope that's the way it went down." He chewed on the side of his thumb, deep lines bracketing his mouth.

"You hope? How is that in any way a good scenario?"

J.D. sat forward, wedging his forearms on his thighs. "Because the alternative is that they somehow knew about the laptop, and how could they know about the laptop unless they were bugging us."

"Bugging us?" Goose bumps raced up her back despite the heat of the room, and she eyed the bag at her feet as if it had just sprouted ears.

"When were we talking about the laptop? In my rental SUV on the way over here."

"But then they would've known Tara had my truck, and they would've known I wasn't in it when she pulled into the ranch."

"So? They weren't after you at that point. They figured they'd check the truck for the laptop and if it wasn't there, they'd break into your house again while we were gone."

"And if they put some kind of listening device in your truck, maybe they put a GPS monitor on it at the same time."

He shook his head. "I don't know when they would've had time to do that. The only time the SUV was out of my sight was when I parked it in front of your house when I brought you home. I think we would've noticed a couple of men out front tinkering with my rental car."

Noelle cleared her throat. "We were busy at the time."

"You're right." He raised a brow in her direction. "During our, uh, interlude, I wouldn't have noticed a 747 landing in your driveway."

She pinned her hands between her knees. He'd admitted he'd been totally focused on her while she'd been focused on…a rug. "Then they could've done it."

"I'll give it a sweep when we get back inside."

"However they figured out to nab the laptop, I'm so grateful they didn't hurt Tara. I couldn't take having three…" She broke off, a flush creeping from her chest to her face under his dark gaze.

"I'm glad Tara's safe, but this still means Zendaris may have gotten those plans back. And if he did? The U.S. military can say goodbye to one of the most effective weapons we have against terrorists."

"It's all supposition, J.D. We have no idea whether or not Abby loaded that file on my laptop."

"I guess only time will tell."

"You mean we have to wait until our drone fleet starts mysteriously falling out of the sky?"

"I mean, we'll know as soon as the threats against you stop."

That little flare of hope danced in her chest, and she folded her arms across it. Besides, did she really believe J.D. would be hanging around Buck Ridge with her once Zendaris's men absconded with the plans?

She'd shut him down when he'd been naked, ready and willing to take her for his own. Why would he want to sign up for more of the same? He'd probably be more than happy to go off and chase arms dealers and terrorists in some other part of the world. A warmer part.

Some other woman probably needed saving—one who would more than welcome him in her arms and in her bed.

"Hey."

He squeezed her knee, and she jumped.

"None of this is your fault. Abby involved you in her scheme when she had no right to drag you into this. According to my buddy Cade Stark, that woman was seven kinds of crazy."

"And I'm one." Noelle blinked back the tears. Her vision blurred so that J.D. turned into a dark shape moving into her space.

His warm body squeezed in next to her in the chair, his arm snaking around her shoulders. He pressed his lips against the bandage on her temple. "If you're crazy, half the people I know are raving lunatics. I don't know one woman and only a handful of men who could've endured what you've been through and still be standing, walking, talking and even reasoning like you've been. Okay, that sounded kind of sexist, but you know what I mean."

She allowed her head to drop to his broad shoulder. "When Alex was murdered in front of me, I went into this downward spiral of obsessive-compulsive behavior. My mother was OCD, and I'd had some tendencies over the years, but I think my art saved me. But when Alex died, the guilt was overwhelming."

"A lot of survivors experience guilt. Hell, it's a full-time occupation in my business."

"It was more than survivor's guilt." He opened his mouth to protest again, and she placed a finger over his lips. "You don't understand, J.D. By the time Alex was murdered, I had already asked him for a divorce. I was done with that marriage. We were talking things out. He didn't want a divorce, and he promised things would be better. Then he died, and I didn't have to argue with him anymore—and I got life-insurance money."

His hand slipped to her back and he rubbed circles on her sweater. "A lot of couples fight. A lot of couples get divorced. Just because your husband died at the time you two were having trouble doesn't make it your fault."

"It felt like my fault, and the guilt drove me to extraordinary means to try to control my world."

"But you worked your way out of it."

She guffawed, half laugh, half sob. "That's what you call working my way out of it? I'm buck naked with a hot guy who's doing unbelievably hot things to my body and I'm trying to straighten a *rug?*"

"It's not like you weren't responding to those hot things I was doing to your body." He chuckled softly in her ear, while his hand crept beneath her sweater and thermal top and flattened against her bare back.

"Because even if your mind was thinking about that ripple in the rug, your body was heating up under my fingers." Those same fingers walked to the band of her snow pants and thermals and slipped inside to tease the upper curve of her buttocks.

"My lips." He laid a path of kisses along her hairline.

"My tongue." His tongue dipped into her ear.

"And my..." He made a slight turn in the chair to press against her thigh.

She closed her eyes, a soft sigh escaping her lips. She should be thinking about Zendaris searching through the files on her laptop, but if J.D. could take a break from his spying to tickle her...fancy, she could take a break to savor his attentions.

"Sorry I took so long."

Noelle opened one eye and even that took a Herculean effort as she tried to shake off the sweet languor that had invaded every cell of her body.

Tara had the good grace to sport two red spots on her cheeks for interrupting. "Or maybe I should've taken longer."

J.D. recovered first, adjusting his position in the chair and crossing one booted ankle over his knee. "How'd it go with Sheriff Greavy? Were you able to give him a better description of the men?"

"No." She collapsed in the chair recently vacated by J.D. "Honestly, all I remember is the gun pointing in my face. I could describe that in minute detail."

"I'm so sorry, Tara." Noelle had found her tongue after losing J.D.'s.

"You have no reason to be sorry. I should be apologizing to you since I couldn't safeguard your laptop."

"I can give you a ride back to your ranch in my truck. When's yours going to be ready?"

"Zach said he could have it for me tomorrow." Tara curled one leg beneath her. "In all the excitement back at the sheriff's station, I didn't get a chance to tell you how sorry I am about your friend. Ted told me about Bruce."

"It's terrible. I hope his family can get some answers."

Tara propped a boot on the table between the two chairs. "I'm not comparing what happened to me today to what happened to your friend, but there's a lot of bad stuff going on right now. The air is heavy with...portent."

Noelle nodded as she slipped her hand through the crook of J.D.'s arm.

Tara's eyes popped. "No clicking tongues or rolling eyes?"

J.D. asked, "What does that mean?"

"I have feelings sometimes. I think it's my Native American heritage. I'm highly attuned to the universe." She tapped her chest with a fist. "Usually, Noelle laughs at me, snorts or rolls her eyes, and sometimes she does all three at once. Now you're agreeing with me?"

"Even I can't deny there's something in the air. I can't feel it like you can, but I can see it happening with my own eyes—J.D.'s accident with the truck, your holdup and, of course, Bruce's death. I hope it ends soon." She just might get her wish if Zendaris found the plans on her laptop.

Tara clapped her mittened hands together. "Finally—acknowledgment."

"Unless you ladies want to eat here or get something to drink, I think we'd better head out before the next storm moves in."

"Yeah, we'd better get moving." Tara yawned. "I told Mom I was hung up, didn't mention a word about the masked gunmen. She'd freak out."

J.D. eased out of the chair, and Noelle immediately missed the press of his body against hers. How was she going to feel when he walked out of her life forever?

Noelle grabbed her jacket and shook it out. "Did you park by the sheriff's substation?"

"Yeah. Are you parked there, too?"

"Uh-huh." Noelle held out her hand. "Keys? I'll drive."

Tara hugged her purse to her chest. "Are you sure? Aren't you still recovering from your concussion and that bump on your head?"

"I'm going to have to drive it from your place to mine anyway, and it's not like I'm going to go out and play football. I had a concussion. It's over. Now give me the keys."

"Is she a hard taskmaster at the ranch, too?" Tara jabbed J.D. with her elbow.

"At the ranch?"

Narrowing her eyes, Tara said, "You know, at the ranch where you're *working?*"

"Yeah. Oh, yeah. She keeps me on my toes."

Tara dropped her gaze to J.D.'s cowboy boots. "Yeah, right."

"Would you stop grilling J.D. and start walking toward the parking lot?"

Once they hit the parking lot by the sheriff's substation, Noelle grabbed her friend's arm and pulled her toward the truck parked five spaces from J.D.'s rental SUV.

"I'll be right behind you all the way," J.D. called as he slipped into his car.

When they got in the truck and Noelle turned the ignition, Tara turned to her. "What's really going on between you and J.D.?"

"What do you mean?" Noelle idled at the exit, waiting for J.D.'s headlights to pull up behind them.

"He doesn't seem like your average ranch hand. Why is he by your side every minute of the day like some kind of protective pit bull?"

"You think he's being protective?" Noelle pulled onto the road with J.D. trailing after her—just the way she liked it—her pit bull.

"Well, yeah. The way he hovers over you, touches your hand. The way he looks at you, for goodness' sakes."

"Maybe he's just madly in love with me. I have that effect on men."

"The effect you've had on men is as their caretaker. Let's face it—Alex hitched his star to yours because he knew a good thing when he saw it. But that J.D. is different."

Was he ever. "In what way?"

Noelle already knew the answer. She just wanted to hear Tara say it. She just wanted someone else to confirm it for her, so she'd know she wasn't dreaming.

"*He's* the caretaker. That man doesn't need looking after. I think it's good for you. Maybe you can let go a little bit now."

"He's just a hired hand, Tara. We're not having a relationship."

"If you say so." She dug into her purse and pulled out

a bag from the pharmacy. "At least I picked up your prescription."

Tara dropped the bag on the console, and then she zipped her lip for the rest of the ride home, resting her head against the back of her seat and closing her eyes.

Thank God Zendaris's thugs had been interested in the computer only and hadn't harmed Tara. Noelle couldn't take being the cause of one more person's injuries—or death.

She turned onto Tara's property and pulled up to the house with J.D. idling behind her. "Are you going to be okay?"

Tara opened the door of the truck and swung around so that her legs dangled toward the running board. "I'm going to hit the tub and soak in some hot water with a glass of wine. You?"

"I just might do the same."

"Then let J.D. scrub your back."

"Is that metaphorically speaking?"

"No. I mean let him scrub your back." She hopped down from the truck and waved.

Noelle watched Tara slip into her house before making a wide turn and leaving the property. J.D.'s headlights burned brightly behind her.

Of course she wouldn't be asking him to scrub her back. She couldn't get any more involved with him than she already was. If she came to depend on him in any way, once he left she'd be scrambling to pick up the pieces. And she knew what that meant for her mental well-being.

She turned into her ranch and fear fluttered in her belly. The men who'd been tracking her for over two weeks now had felt comfortable enough coming onto her property and holding her friend at gunpoint. What would stop them from coming back if they wanted to?

Throwing the truck into Park, she glanced in her rear-view mirror. J.D. would stop them. J.D. and the fact that they had her laptop and possibly those plans they'd been searching for.

The idea that there were enemies in the world who were actively seeking to destroy America's capability to strike at them terrified her. Even living in D.C., she didn't want to know about such things. People like her trusted men and women like J.D. to keep them safe. People like her just didn't want to know the details of what that involved.

J.D. was by her side when she hit the bottom step of her dismantled porch. She pointed to the plywood. "When are you going to fix this? I should start paying you by the hour, you know."

"You *should* start paying me."

"Did you sweep the SUV for bugs?"

"I didn't find anything. My guess is they saw your truck with a woman climbing inside, made their move, realized their mistake and then got lucky by noticing the laptop. Now maybe *we'll* get lucky and there will be nothing on that laptop but the notes of an artist."

"Then we'll all be back to square one—Zendaris believing I know something about the plans and me running from him. When will we all be safe?"

"When Zendaris and every man like him is dead."

She shrugged out of her jacket and hung it on the hook. "Are you hungry? I can make something simple."

"Let me do it. You go relax."

The hot bath beckoned. Maybe she should try a glass of wine with it. She didn't plan on taking any medication. She just wanted it for insurance in case the OCD flared up again.

"Maybe I'll soak in the tub."

"Good idea. I have a few phone calls to make. I have to

give my boss the bad news that I may have lost the plans to Zendaris again."

"We still don't know if the plans were even on my laptop. And if they are, will Zendaris's guys be able to figure out how to locate them? I'm sure Abby didn't call the file Top Secret Anti-Drone Plans."

"Believe me, Zendaris may have sent a couple of killers after you to take care of business, but one or both of those killers will also have computer skills, weapons skills, electronics skills. He hires only the best."

She shook her head. "I can't believe there are that many people out there in the world with the skills and the motivation to do such harm."

"Hate to burst your bubble, darlin', but there are." He pulled his phone from his pocket. "You go take that bath, and I'll make my calls. I'll have some eggs or pasta ready for you when you come out. And, Noelle?"

"Yes?"

"Leave your phone here. If you don't mind, I'm going to attach a GPS tracking device to it. I don't want to lose you again."

She froze. Alex had kept tabs on her, too, but his motivations had been a lot different from J.D.'s. She shrugged. "Knock yourself out."

She closed the bathroom door and cranked on the faucets in the tub. She dumped some bath salts into the steaming water and then shed her clothes, leaving them in a pile on the floor.

She dipped a toe in the water first and swirled it around before easing her entire body into the tub. The hot water lapped around her legs, and she slumped farther down to allow the shallow water to warm her chilled skin.

Now that Zendaris had her laptop and possibly the plans he'd been seeking, would Prospero give J.D. orders to find a way to get to Zendaris and retrieve the plans? Was J.D.'s boss giving him those orders right now?

Tomorrow this could all be a bad memory. Both Zendaris and J.D. would be out of her life, and she could get back to the business of sprucing up the ranch.

Maybe now that the dark threat hanging over her no longer existed, she could return to D.C. and leave the ranch to Ted. If he really was clean and sober, he could make a life here, and she could give him that chance. She wanted to give him that chance.

The water had crept up to her shoulders, and she drew her knees up to her chest to cool off. She closed her eyes and cupped puddles of the silky liquid in her hands and dumped them on her knees.

If J.D. disappeared from her life tomorrow, she wanted one night with him before he left—one night to remind her that she was alive and could continue to live without all the guilt weighing her down and restricting her.

If she could make love one night with abandon, she could vanquish all the ghosts that haunted her and the memory of that night in the art gallery when Alex had tried to sacrifice her to save his own life.

She shuddered and slid farther into the warm embrace of the lavender-scented water. She'd never told anyone the details of that night except Dr. Eliason, although the cops had seen it all on the security video.

She'd joined Alex in the gallery at closing time to give him a ride home since they had just one car between them. He'd been running late, as usual, so she'd parked and gone into the gallery. He should've secured the back door.

But he hadn't.

The masked men came through the back, surprising both of them. One of them ordered Alex to open the safe. Instead, Alex got the bright idea of escaping. As he ran for the front doors, the thieves ordered him to stop and trained their guns on him.

Instead of stopping, Alex had grabbed her and held her in front of him as a shield. The gunman killed Alex anyway. As he fell to the ground, he took her with him.

The robbers left her alive—probably figured she'd suffered enough that night since her own husband had tried to use her to protect himself.

So why did the guilt follow *her* around? Dr. Eliason had told her she'd rationalized Alex's behavior that night because she'd been the one who'd wanted out of the marriage. As if endangering someone's life to save your own was just punishment for wanting a divorce.

Sighing, she sat up and the water sluiced off her body. She'd been going over the same stuff for two years—time to put it behind her and move forward. What better way to do that than with a new man—even if that man was hers for only one more day?

She toweled off and slipped into some flannel pajamas. Not the sexiest getup for a seduction, but she didn't want any game playing between her and J.D. tonight. She wanted him because she wanted him, because she'd missed her chance earlier that day.

She stuck her head out of the bathroom and sniffed the air. The lavender steam mingled with the smell of garlic coming from the kitchen.

She scooped up her clothes from the bathroom and dumped them on the floor of her bedroom. There—she was starting already. She didn't need to hang up the clothes right away. They'd still be there when she went to bed.

"Something smells good in here." She joined J.D. in the kitchen, where he had garlic and tomatoes sizzling in a pan of olive oil.

"Nothing fancy. The spaghetti's almost done." He tapped

a bottle of wine on the counter. "Thought we could use a glass of wine or two if you have a corkscrew."

"You must've read my mind." She reached around him for the utensil drawer and pulled out a corkscrew.

While she opened the wine, he took the boiling spaghetti off the stove and dumped it into a colander in the sink. They loaded up their plates, grabbed a couple of bowls for salad and headed for the kitchen table.

"Sorry, no time to set the table."

She poured him a glass of red wine. "Did you talk to Prospero?"

"I did."

"And?"

"I guess we'll know soon enough if the plans were on the laptop—not that Zendaris will send us an email or anything. So we still need to remain vigilant until we know one way or the other."

Noelle's heart did a somersault. Did this mean J.D. would be sticking around?

"If the plans are on my laptop, then I apologize for not thinking of that possibility sooner."

"Not. Your. Fault." He clinked his wineglass with hers. "We should've figured out that one ourselves. We're supposed to be the professionals, not you. Abby was a computer whiz. It would make sense she'd hide the plans on a computer. We just never figured she'd relinquish control over those plans by putting them on someone else's computer. It's like you said before. You could've done anything with that laptop."

"Yeah, I lost it." Noelle twirled some spaghetti around her fork, picking up bits of garlic and tomato in the process.

"Bad timing all around. Once it's safe, are you going to go back to D.C. or hang around here?"

Where will you be?

She stuffed the forkful of spaghetti in her mouth and chewed to keep from blurting out something she'd regret. She swallowed, dabbed her mouth with a napkin and took a sip of wine.

"I might stay here since I took a leave of absence from my job. I'm thinking about turning the ranch over to Ted."

"Do you really think that's a good idea? He seems kind of unstable."

"Well, hopefully that's in the past. Maybe he just needs something and someplace to get stable."

Her cell phone buzzed beside her on the table, and she glanced at the display. "Speak of the devil, and I mean that in the nicest way."

She slid the phone toward her and pressed the button to read Ted's text. "He sent me a picture."

She brought the phone closer to her face to peer at the image. Blood pounded against the wound on her head and she gripped the edge of the table with one hand as the room spun out of control.

J.D. reached out a hand, knocking over her glass. The wine spread on the white tablecloth like blood.

"Noelle, what is it?"

"They got Ted…and this time they have the right guy."

Chapter Sixteen

J.D. lunged across the table and knocked over his own wine, the spreading stain matching the one from Noelle's glass. He plucked the phone from Noelle's hand.

The image on the screen showed Ted, bound and gagged.

Clutching the phone in his hand, he knelt beside Noelle's chair. Her face had gone as white as the tablecloth had been before the twin blotches had marred it.

"There's no message attached to the picture. We don't know what this is."

She turned wide violet eyes on him that seemed to take up half her face. "What else could it possibly mean? Ted would not send me a picture of himself tied up and gagged. This isn't a joke."

"What does it mean? Why would they want your brother when they have the laptop?" The cell phone vibrated in his hand.

They were about to find out.

He pushed the button to open the text and read it out loud. "'We have your brother. We need you.'"

Noelle choked.

"They're not getting you. Do you understand me?" He grabbed her hands, now stiff and cold.

Noelle stared at the buzzing phone.

"Answer it," J.D. whispered.

Her hand trembled as she took it from his palm.

He encircled her wrist. "Put it on speaker."

She answered the phone and thumbed the button for the speaker. "H-hello?"

"Are you alone?"

Her gaze shifted to J.D.'s face and he gave a slight nod. "Yes."

"Doesn't matter anyway. If anyone helps you, your brother is dead. Did you like the picture?"

The voice, slightly accented, didn't mock, didn't tease, which almost made the question more chilling.

"Is he hurt? Did you hurt him?"

"No. His companion for the evening slipped something in his drink. As your brother faded out, he assumed he was going to wake up in the arms of the lovely Pia. He woke up, just in different circumstances. He's fine."

The woman at the Buck Ridge Lodge?

J.D. circled his finger in the air to get Noelle talking again. They had to find out as much as they could while they had this guy on the line.

"What do you want from me? You have my laptop. I swear I don't know anything."

"I think we've come to that realization, but now we need to get into the file Abby put on your computer—and you're going to help us."

"If she put something on my laptop and you have the laptop, then just open it."

The man tsked. "It's not that easy. Our Abby was a computer genius, wasn't she? She put safeguards on this file."

"Don't you people do this sort of thing for a living? You can't crack a password on a file? Abby once told me it was easy to do."

"This is a different kind of password. We need your voice."

J.D. swore under his breath. That Abby Warren was a piece of work. She'd involved Noelle at every level.

Noelle dug her fingernails into the denim covering his leg and hunched her shoulders. She hadn't realized the full implications of the password.

"I don't understand. Why do you need my voice?"

"Your clever roommate installed a voice-activated password on this file. We need you to say the code into the microphone of this laptop to unlock the file."

"Are you kidding me?" The nails dug deeper. "I don't know what you're talking about. I don't know any voice-activated…"

She released her grip on his thigh and covered her mouth.

The man on the phone pounced. "You do know it, don't you? Abby would've had you say something into the mic to set this up."

"I don't remember." She shook her head at J.D. "I don't remember what it is. She did have me read a set of words or names into the microphone, but she told me it was just a test. She didn't install the voice-activated security on any of my own files."

"You'd better remember, and we're here to help you remember. We have your brother, Noelle. We'll kill him if you don't join us and unlock this file. Then we'll kill you and that cowboy bodyguard you have hanging around you every minute of the day."

Noelle swallowed.

"Come alone. Tomorrow night. You unlock this file and we'll be out of your life, and you can take your brother with you."

"What's in the file?"

"You don't need to worry about that. Secrets. Every country has them. *I* don't even know what's in the file. I just have orders from my superior to get it. You and I? We don't need to concern ourselves with all of that."

"Where are you? Where do you have Ted?"

"Oh, no. It's not going to be that easy. We give you our location and you tell the sheriff or the cowboy and we get ambushed. A few of us will pick you up, and the rest will stay with your brother. That way, if anything unplanned happens to us, the others will execute your brother."

J.D. squeezed her wrist and mouthed *No*.

She shook him off. "Where? Where will you pick me up?"

"We'll be in touch."

The phone went dead, and Noelle dropped it onto the table. "What are we going to do?"

"We're going to wait for further instructions on the meeting place tomorrow, and then I'm going to go out there like the welcoming committee from hell."

The adrenaline was already coursing through his veins at the thought of getting close to Zendaris's men.

"You can't do that, J.D. You heard him. They'll kill Ted."

"You don't think they're going to kill him anyway, and you, if you go out there? You don't even know the pass-word, and you don't want to know how they plan to get it out of you."

"So you go to the meeting place instead of me and start shooting? Then what? The people holding Ted will know. They'll kill him. And what about me? What if you die instead? What happens to me then?" Her words ended on a sob.

He dropped to his knees in front of her and wrapped his arms around her waist. "I'm not going to die. Trust me. I can get other agents out here for backup. We can save Ted, too."

"Other agents?" She touched his face. "How long is that going to take? They have Ted."

"Even if they can't get here tomorrow night, we have a lot of time. They need your voice to unlock that file. They're not going to hurt Ted before you get there. We can do this. Prospero can do this. We've been waiting four long years for another crack at Zendaris."

"What if I go first as the bait, and then you and your agents follow me in?"

"No. I don't want you anywhere near these guys. We'll figure out something."

She blinked her long, dark lashes. "A-are you sure?"

"I'm positive, darlin'. We can do this." His skin prickled as a warm flush stole over his body. It was the adrenaline high he always got before a mission.

If they captured even one of Zendaris's men it would be the biggest lead they'd had in the four years since they had disrupted his first major arms deal. They needed this win.

Noelle's fingers tangled in his hair, and she cupped his jaw. "I trust you, J.D. I know you want to bring this guy down."

"And keep you safe. I want to keep you safe, Noelle." He turned his head to kiss the inside of her palm.

The phone vibrated, and she swept it from the table.

J.D.'s muscles coiled. "Is it them?"

"No. Just Tara checking up on me."

She pocketed the phone. Leaning forward, she wrapped her arms around his shoulders. "Tell me this is going to be okay."

"We've got this, Noelle." He pressed his face between her breasts and inhaled her sweet scent.

She hooked her arms around his neck and drew him even closer.

He raised his head and kissed the base of her throat,

where her pulse thudded. He didn't want to rush into anything this time. Fear had driven her into his arms again, and, while he wanted to be here for her, he'd try to contain his desire this time.

Resting her chin on the top of his head, she sighed. "I just want you to hold me. This could be our last night..."

He drew back from her and pinched her chin, pressing his thumb against her bottom lip. "Once we put an end to this threat against you and turn the tables on Zendaris, you and I will have a lot of nights together."

Her eyes widened, and he felt as if he could drown in their depths. He couldn't wait to make love with her with all the barriers between them cleared away—but that moment would come later.

"You want to continue this—" one hand fluttered in the air "—what we have between us?"

"Am I out of line?" If she started lining up forks or whatever, he'd spoken too soon.

"N-no. I want a chance to get to know you without the constant drama."

"Exactly. We're going to rescue Ted and keep you out of Zendaris's clutches. I'm even confident we can get that laptop back in our hands."

"Must be nice to have so much confidence." She cradled his face in her hands. "It even rubs off on me."

"Good." He jerked his thumb over his shoulder. "Do you want me to get a fire going? We can discuss our plan for tomorrow, and maybe that plan will start with stalling Zendaris's men."

"And women?" She picked up the two wineglasses that had fallen onto the table and set them on their bases. "Did you catch that? The woman who drugged Ted could've been the one at the lodge that night."

"It wasn't or she would've known Ted instead of Bruce

was your brother, so stop thinking you should've known the redhead was evil." He pushed to his feet and checked the wood in the basket by the fireplace.

"You get the fire started, and I'm going to refill our wineglasses. I'm feeling relatively calm, given the circumstances, and I want to remain that way before I start organizing books again."

"You're doing great, Noelle, and you do have a measure of control over this situation. You're going to help me figure out how to stall these guys until the Prospero cavalry arrives."

He stacked the wood on the grate while she clinked glasses in the kitchen and cleared off the table.

By the time she returned with two full glasses of wine, he'd swung the love seat in front of the fire again and plumped a pillow against the back cushion. He patted the pillow. "Have a seat. I need some of that wine or I'll never be able to sleep tonight—too much excitement."

"I could tell the prospect of meeting up with these people face-to-face gave you a buzz." She placed the wineglasses on the table and sank onto the love seat.

"That obvious, huh? I hope you don't think I'm happy about it. It's the nature of the job. These are the moments we train for."

"I understand." She handed him a glass and crossed her legs beneath her. "I just want to get Ted back safely. It seems that he's always suffered because of me."

"Noelle." God, he hated it when she started blaming herself for every bad thing that happened to someone close to her.

"Don't worry. I'm not going down that road." She swirled the dark red liquid in her glass. "I'm not saying I'm the cause of Ted's suffering, but my existence as the favored child, the legal child in the family, wasn't easy for him."

J.D. took a swig of his wine.

She dipped her head to his shoulder, and he smoothed the hair back from her face. He didn't believe for one minute this would be their last night together, but if she thought that and it drove her back into his arms, he'd take it. Slowly.

"Do you want some more wine?"

"I'm okay."

"I need another, and I hate drinking alone. One more." She placed a hand flat on his belly. "You still seem all keyed up to me."

Did she think he was a jerk for getting pumped up about this confrontation? It wasn't as if Ted's kidnapping made him happy. But now that it had happened, he couldn't wait to get his hands on a couple of Zendaris's people.

He had to show her he could relax, too. He downed the last sip of cabernet and held out his glass. "Sure. One more."

She grabbed her own glass from the floor and headed back to the kitchen. "So what's the plan for tomorrow?"

"The first thing we do is stall, so we can get some backup."

"Do you think they'll hurt Ted?"

"No. They need you. If they don't have Ted or they injure him, you're not going to cooperate. They have you right where they want you, but they didn't count on the full force of Prospero dropping on them like a hammer."

She returned, carrying two full glasses of wine. She handed one to him and cradled her own with two hands.

"So I'm going to stall them when they call back with instructions."

He sipped the wine. Its warmth seemed to bring him down a few notches. Noelle was right. He needed to unwind. He took another sip.

"Yeah, stall. Tell them you can't get away from me, that if you go out to meet them I'll follow you."

"They'll believe that." She put the wine to her lips and her eyes glowed over the rim of the glass. "They'll think getting to Zendaris is more important to you than saving my brother."

"Exactly." His head dropped back against the love-seat cushion, and then lolled to the side. It was almost too much effort to lift it. The heat from the fire and the warmth from the wine had woven a sleepy spell around him.

It's a good thing he didn't have any plans for Noelle tonight since he doubted he could make it to the bedroom at this point.

"You tired?" His lids felt heavy as he looked at her, and he blinked his dry eyes.

"It's been a long day." She took the glass from his limp fingers before he could drop it. "We should go to sleep."

"Sleep?" He tried to turn his wrist to look at his watch, but the motor skills required to do that wouldn't obey his brain. "It's surly."

Surly? His tongue felt thick. He felt...drugged.

NOELLE TUCKED A pillow behind J.D.'s head. If he had to sleep sitting upright, she wanted to make sure he didn't wake up with a stiff neck—especially if he planned to come to her rescue.

Reaching down, she picked up her full wineglass and hurried to the kitchen, carrying J.D.'s half-empty glass as well. She peered into the swirling red liquid—no hint of the small white pills she'd crushed and dissolved in the wine.

She dumped the contents down the drain and ran the water. Even though he hadn't finished the entire glass of wine, he just needed to be under long enough for her to escape the house and be on her way to the meeting with Ted's kidnappers.

She couldn't wait. She couldn't do this on J.D.'s terms. He didn't understand. She couldn't be responsible for another death.

But he'd still get a shot at Zendaris's flunkies.

She ripped a sheet of paper from the notepad by the phone and scribbled on it. She secured the note on the coffee table with J.D.'s empty wineglass. He should have no problem seeing that when he came to. She just hoped she hadn't drugged him too heavily.

She dried her hands on a paper towel and tiptoed to the front door, where she lifted her jacket from a hook. She'd give them their stupid password and then grab Ted and get out of there. Maybe by that time, J.D. would be on his way.

Why wouldn't they let her go? What was she going to do, report them to the small-town sheriff? They'd figure they would be long gone before she returned to the ranch or town to tell anyone.

Prospero could regroup and take the plans back, or that scientist who developed the anti-drone could develop an anti-anti-drone. This sort of thing must go on all the time.

She squeezed her eyes shut to burn those justifications into her brain. She didn't want to make it any easier for arms dealers and terrorists to ply their deadly trade, but she had to save Ted. And she just might end up saving J.D., too.

Clutching her jacket to her chest, she crept back to the love seat. His face, which had been tight with nervous energy, had relaxed and the lines had melted away. Leaning forward, she kissed his brow, then his mouth.

She whispered, "I hope we have a chance to figure out all this between us—unless you can't forgive me for messing up your plans. But for once, I needed to take control and make my own plans."

She backed away from him and spun toward the front door, tears blurring her vision. She snapped the door behind her and climbed into her truck.

The text she'd received earlier, and had hidden from J.D., had instructed her to drive north on the highway until she got to the fifteen-mile marker. Then she was supposed to park and wait.

She pulled away from the ranch and the half-finished porch. Would J.D. stay to complete it? Would she live to see it completed?

The fifteen-mile marker came too soon, and she pulled into the turnout just as a light snow began to drift from the sky. She cut the engine and the lights and placed both hands on the steering wheel, waiting.

The car slipped up behind her, emerging seamlessly from the snow. She had her instructions.

Grabbing her purse from the seat beside her, she shouldered open the door of the truck and planted one booted foot on the icy gravel.

The car flashed its lights once, and she headed for the twin beams skewering the night. She trudged up to the left-rear door of the Jeep and tugged on the handle.

When the door swung open, warmth and the scent of that now-familiar men's cologne wafted from the interior.

"Get in."

She recognized the voice from the phone. She dropped to the leather seat, her upper arm bumping the gun trained on her.

She gasped and jerked away.

The driver adjusted the rearview mirror, and she met his gaze, peering at her from a slit in a black ski mask—just like the ones Alex's killers had worn. "Don't worry, Noelle. We're not going to hurt you…unless someone followed you."

"Nobody followed me."

The low rumble of the engine roared to life and the car crawled past her truck. The front passenger window whisked down and the driver leaned across the seat and pointed at a dark object out the window.

The truck seemed to implode and disintegrate, and Noelle didn't hear a thing. The only sign that a two-ton vehicle had been parked there was a smoldering heap of scrap metal and a gust of black smoke fighting to rise through the snow.

Zendaris obviously made good use of the high-tech weapons he bought and sold in hotel rooms, caves and presidential palaces.

The driver chuckled. "I can tell by your reaction there was no one in the truck. We're off to a great start."

"Have you hurt my brother?"

"Your brother may have been a little hurt to discover the woman with whom he'd been sharing his nights wanted something more than his body, but other than that—" his shoulders rose and fell "—he's fine."

"I'm just warning you now. I don't remember any verbal password. I do remember a series of words, names and phrases Abby had me speak into the computer mic, but that was almost six months ago."

"We have ways of…helping you remember."

"I don't think you're going to torture it out of me." She shoved her hands in her pockets so the gun-wielding passenger beside her couldn't see them tremble.

"Torture?" He clicked his tongue. "You've been listening to your cowboy bodyguard too much. Who is he?"

She may have just drugged J.D. and ruined his chances of getting closer to Zendaris, but she had no intention of outing him.

"He's an old friend of the family, a former marine who's

been drifting the past few years. He just came along at the right time."

"Or the wrong time. If he tries to follow you, we'll kill him."

"He's not going to follow me. He doesn't know where I am. He doesn't know about this meeting. I didn't want to put anyone else in jeopardy."

"Good." He cranked the wheel to the right, and the truck bounced over the rough terrain. The four-wheel drive kicked in and the wheels dug in and churned over the snow-dappled access road.

Noelle spied a light in the distance. As they drew closer, a small cabin emerged along the tree line.

The truck pulled behind the cabin next to a small helicopter. Noelle's stomach dropped. If they took her away in a helicopter it wouldn't matter that J.D. had a GPS tracking device on her phone. He'd never get to her in time to capture Zendaris's men.

The driver got out first. He opened her door with one hand while training a small gun at her chest—at least it looked small after that weapon he'd poked out the window to disintegrate her truck.

She clambered out of the truck, and her silent companion in the back followed her out. Now she had two guns pointed at her by two masked men. It wasn't as if she hadn't been in this situation before.

They marched her into the cabin, and she breathed a sigh of relief. No helicopter ride tonight—at least not yet.

The taller man shoved open the door and pushed her across the threshold.

"Ted!" She stumbled across the carpeted floor of the cabin toward her brother; his hands were tied behind his back, his ankles roped to a chair.

"What kind of mess have you gotten yourself into, Noelle? I thought *I* was the unstable one in this family."

She dropped to her knees in front of him, ignoring the blonde standing to his right. She was the only one unmasked, but then, Ted already knew what she looked like. "Are you okay? Did they hurt you?"

He eyed his captors through narrowed eyes. "Not yet. What the hell do they want from you, and why the hell are you here? Not to save my sorry ass?"

"My roommate, Abby, put something on my laptop and they want it."

"That's enough. He doesn't need to know any more." The woman stepped from the shadows, the low light in the cabin gleaming in her blond hair.

Noelle sat back on her heels. "Why don't you let him go as a sign of good faith? You have me here now, and I'll help you access the file...if I can."

Everyone seemed to say no at the same time, including Ted. Maybe her brother had changed—just in time.

"We call the shots here, Noelle." The driver of the car rubbed his hands together. "And right now we need to unlock that file."

She pushed to her feet and lurched toward the desk, where her laptop glowed in the dimly lit room. "I'm ready to try."

The man with the accent pulled out the chair and gestured to it with a sweep of his hand. "Have a seat."

Noelle perched on the edge of the hard chair, facing her computer. They'd opened a folder she'd never seen before, which contained one document. The document's title contained only digits, which looked random. They must've known how to search for the contents of the file. The document icon sported a tiny microphone, which must indicate a voice password-protected file.

Abby had been clever. She'd told Noelle she was developing some new computer technology and had her sit in front of the laptop recording different words and sounds. If only she could remember some of those words, phrases and names now.

Licking her lips, she slid a gaze to the man in the ski mask. What if she just deleted the file? She could save Prospero a lot of time and effort.

Of course, she'd probably get herself and Ted killed. But would that happen anyway? J.D. seemed to think so, and he knew these people better than she did.

Her hand swooped for the mouse and right-clicked on the file.

A stinging blow hit the back of her head, and her eyes watered.

"Nobody told you to touch that file. You do something like that again and we'll shoot Ted." To drive home this threat, the big man who'd been in the backseat with her released the safety on his weapon with a click that resounded through the cabin.

Noelle clasped her hands in her lap. "What do you want me to do?"

"Start that brain of yours working. At any time did Abby record your voice?"

She had, but Noelle didn't want to give these guys any more than she had to.

"Maybe. Maybe she did it without my knowledge."

"It would've been at the computer. When you were sitting at your laptop, did she have you say any words?"

Tilting her head, she wrapped her hair around one hand. "Maybe."

That one word earned her another slap on the back of her head. She gulped back a sob. J.D. had been right. These people would never let her and Ted live, whether or not she got them into the file.

But at least Ted wouldn't suffer alone. At least she'd tried to save him.

"I'm thinking." She rubbed the back of her head. "Stop hitting me. It's not helping."

"Think harder."

Noelle squeezed her eyes shut. What had Abby told her to repeat? Nonsense words, mostly. How would she ever remember a bunch of nonsense words? Some of the word combinations had been names, but they weren't celebrity names or names of anyone she knew.

Her eyes flew open. J.D.'s voice filtered into her mind, his words swirling in her head. He'd told her more than she'd ever known about Abby Warren, told her of Abby's obsession, told her the name of Abby's obsession.

The hulk moved behind her, his cologne overpowering her senses. Curving his arm around her neck, he showed her the long syringe between his fingers. "We can help you remember, Noelle. We can help you remember a lot of things."

Her nostrils flared. If they injected her with truth serum, they might get more than they bargained for—like the identity of her cowboy bodyguard.

She had to give them the name. She had to give them the password she'd remembered.

Or they'd never let J.D. leave Buck Ridge alive.

Chapter Seventeen

J.D. smacked his lips and groaned. His tongue felt as if it had doubled in size and he couldn't move it around his dry mouth.

He peeled open his eyes, one at a time, his gaze lazily scanning the room.

He sat forward and nearly toppled over. The last thing he remembered was drinking wine with Noelle beside him, her body ripe for the taking.

Only he was the one who'd been taken.

She'd drugged his wine—and he knew why. That text she'd received earlier hadn't been from Tara. He'd been stupid not to check it himself, but it never occurred to him that she'd go off on her own to meet Zendaris's people.

Or hadn't it?

He knew she felt responsible for the deaths of her husband and Pierpont. She wasn't going to allow Ted's murder to be placed at her doorstep.

She should've trusted him.

How much of a head start had they gotten? He rolled his wrist inward. If they'd gone by helicopter, he'd have a helluva time catching up. Even if they'd taken off in a car, Noelle had already been alone with those maniacs long enough.

He eyed the empty glass of wine on the table in front

of him. It anchored a piece of white paper. He dived for it, crinkling it in his hand.

He rubbed his blurry eyes to read the message. "'Follow my phone.'"

She hadn't been as naive as he feared. He lunged for his own phone and placed the most important call of his life.

On the other end of the line, he heard, "Fifty-eight, sixty-two."

J.D. didn't even know what the digits stood for anymore. He only knew it signaled a secure Prospero connection.

"I need a location on a cell phone."

"Code and GPS tracker, please."

J.D. shook his head, clearing the last wisps of fog shrouding his brain. He repeated his code name and the five-digit number of the tracking device he'd placed on Noelle's cell phone.

After a few minutes and several clicks of a keyboard, the technician came back on the line. "Ready?"

"Go ahead."

"Location, Buck Ridge, Colorado." He rattled off some coordinates.

J.D. punched the coordinates into his phone, which displayed a map of the area. He zoomed in to view the location, and then brought up the directions to it.

He blew out a tense breath and rolled back his shoulders. He'd use the snowmobile to get there the back way, and then he'd have to go in on foot to approach whatever structure he encountered. They had to be someplace with electricity and amenities. They wouldn't be in a cave or in the middle of the woods.

No time for coffee; he downed a can of cola from the fridge and grabbed another on the way out. Noelle hadn't slipped him enough of her meds to keep him out for long. She obviously wanted him to find her, but she'd wanted to do this on her own terms. He just hoped her terms didn't end up with her dead.

His eagerness to locate her had nothing to do with Zendaris or the plans. He had to save Noelle.

A half hour later, the snowmobile vibrated beneath him as he churned through the snow, dodging trees and rocks. His GPS display showed him drawing closer to the location. He couldn't alert Noelle's captors with the whining engine of the snowmobile, so he found a cluster of trees and abandoned the vehicle.

He slogged through the snow along the tree line as white flakes cascaded through the night air. Right now the snow was his friend, muting sounds and obscuring views.

A dark shape materialized along the edge of the trees, a sliver of light seemingly floating on one edge. As he drew closer, the shape became a small, dilapidated cabin, the light a glow from a window.

A figure appeared in front of the cabin and J.D. tensed his muscles. A lookout.

J.D. edged closer and then dropped to the ground. He carved a path through the snow with his body, army-crawling just like in the old days, keeping hidden beneath each snowdrift.

When he got close enough, he took aim with a weapon that shot poison darts. He didn't want to kill the subject, since anyone close to Zendaris was worth questioning.

He shot one dart, then two. The figure dropped to the ground, and J.D. coiled in preparation for a reaction from the cabin. Nothing. They must be busy with something else in there.

Hunching over, he ran toward the body and pulled the person—a woman—next to the cabin so she'd be out of sight. She must be the one who had hooked up with Ted.

He did recon around the perimeter. His gut flipped

when he saw the chopper, but at least it was still parked and not flying off with Noelle. He found a space beneath the front porch that led to a larger crawl space under the cabin itself. He flashed his penlight into the darkness, thankful the dead raccoon he'd just rolled over was frozen into a Popsicle.

Voices. He could hear voices from above.

Shoving through more debris, he followed the sound. Thin shafts of light pierced the crawl space and he made his way toward them. As the light fell across his hands, he blinked and pressed his face against the rotting wood.

His gaze darted back and forth, taking in the small room over his head. He couldn't see all of the inhabitants of the room, but he could hear their voices.

He pulled a knife from his pocket and wedged the blade between two pieces of wood, prying them apart. This gave him a broader view of the room above.

And it didn't look good.

How much longer could she stall? How many more incorrect passwords could she utter before she was locked out of the file? Surely, Abby must've put some limit on the number of failed passwords.

She just might run out before J.D. came to her rescue. Would he even get the hint about the phone?

Her gaze darted toward the front door of the cabin. What could one man alone do to save her and Ted? If she'd gone along with J.D.'s plan, he'd have reinforcements, but she couldn't risk Ted's safety.

With her mouth dry, she intoned another phrase into the computer's mic, knowing it would do nothing to unlock the file and fully aware that it might lock her out for good.

The man with the needle waved it in the air. "She'll

never remember this way, boss. I say we stick her and see what happens."

The larger man had taken to calling the other one *boss*. It also seemed curious that none of them had attempted to contact Zendaris for his take on the situation, and the man with the accent had ordered the blonde to keep watch outside. He seemed accustomed to giving orders.

Was the masked man Zendaris himself?

Noelle cleared her throat. "Zendaris."

The enforcer over her right shoulder grunted and leaned in toward the computer screen. The file didn't open, as she'd known it wouldn't. She just wanted to see their reaction to the name.

The man in charge glided toward her, as stealthy as a panther. "Where did you hear that name?"

"Zendaris?" She shrugged. "It was one of the names Abby had me speak into the computer. It just came to me. You see? I can remember if you give me a chance."

The man's long fingers slid through her hair and then curled around several strands. "Are you sure you heard that name from Abby?"

"Yes? Where else?"

His grip on her hair tightened, and her scalp tingled. "Did the police or…anyone else ever mention that name?"

"No. Now let me keep trying."

"You claimed the man living in your guesthouse was someone from this town."

Knots tightened in her stomach. "A friend of the family, an old boyfriend, actually."

"Why does he carry a gun? How did he know how to detect a hidden camera?"

She snorted. "Are you kidding? A lot of people carry guns out here, and he told me he found the other camera using his cell phone. He's not really a bodyguard or anything. I told you before. He's a former marine. He knows stuff."

The dark eyes in the slits of the mask narrowed, and the room got colder.

Noelle held her breath. She should've never mentioned the name Zendaris. She'd only done so to find out if the man standing to her left, the boss, might be Zendaris.

She'd just gotten her answer.

He snapped his fingers at the other man. "Inject her. I want to get at the truth of a couple of things, not just the password."

With her heart hammering out an irregular staccato, Noelle jumped from her chair, knocking it over.

"Wait! I got this. It must be a name. She had me repeat the names several times. I know. I know the password."

"Don't give it to them, Noelle. They'll kill us both anyway. We might as well die doing something for our country."

Zendaris smacked Ted across the face. "Shut up, pretty boy. I liked you better when you were dumb eye candy, easy for Pia to manipulate."

Now was the time. She had to give them the password or they'd find out about J.D. and his connection to Prospero.

She leaned into the mic and enunciated the name that had come to her an hour ago and had been burning into her brain ever since. "Cade Stark."

The two masked men crowded around the laptop. The file, which had been moved to the computer's desktop, highlighted and then launched.

The sound of splintering wood drowned out the crows of triumph when the file opened.

Noelle spun around in time to see J.D. staggering through the hole he'd just created in the door that led to another room in the cabin.

With his weapon held out, he kicked over Ted's chair and jumped in front of him.

The two men on either side of Noelle scrambled for the guns they'd placed on the table near the computer.

When the noise and dust settled, the three men all had their weapons pointing at each other, and Ted was on his side, still in the chair.

The man Noelle suspected of being Zendaris spoke first. "Bold move for a small-town handyman."

"Are you all right, Noelle?"

"I'm fine, but I had to open the file. I didn't want them to find out that y-you might be on your way."

"I appreciate that, darlin', but do we just let them have that file? It must be mighty important to them if they went through all this trouble to get it."

"Who are you?"

"Like you said, a small-town handyman just trying to protect my old friend. Would you be willing to let us go if we let you take the laptop?"

Noelle swallowed. He couldn't mean that. He'd come too far to give up the file so easily. Her gaze darted to the computer screen, and her jaw dropped.

The enforcer must have looked at the screen the same time she did because he cursed and jabbed the other man in the back.

"Look at the file, boss."

"Keep your gun on him, you idiot." He backed up a few steps and glanced down at the laptop.

He cursed, too, in another language.

With the momentary distraction, adrenaline surged through Noelle's body. She dived under the desk, knocking the chair into the back of Zendaris's knees.

He staggered to the floor, his weapon spinning out of his grasp.

The deafening sound of gunfire erupted in the small space. Someone growled, and she saw the flash of a weapon out of the corner of her eye.

She screamed and flattened herself on the floor. As she lifted her head, she saw the big man push the other man toward the door.

"Get out, boss."

Then he turned his weapon on her.

J.D. lunged toward him.

Noelle screamed. "Go after the other man. It's Zendaris. Go after Zendaris."

The big man roared, "If you follow him, I'll kill her."

J.D. stopped in midstride.

Noelle's heart skipped a beat. He should go after Zendaris. This was his best chance. At least J.D. had a good reason to sacrifice her.

Alex had done it for himself. J.D. would do it for his country.

She squeezed her eyes shut.

The blast of gunfire from two shots echoed in her ears, the smell of gunpowder invading her nostrils. She waited for the pain, the blackness.

"Noelle!"

Strong hands gripped her arms and pulled her from beneath the desk. "Did he shoot you? Are you okay?"

Her eyes flew open. Zendaris's enforcer lay dead on the floor, blood from the wound in his head soaking the dingy carpet.

A cold blast of air gusted in from the front door.

"Go get him. I swear it's Zendaris." She plucked at J.D.'s sleeve.

He crushed her against his chest. "Whether he's Zendaris or not, it doesn't matter anymore. He's gone. I heard the helicopter take off."

She grabbed the front of his jacket. "You should've gone after him. It was your best chance."

"You're my best chance." He cupped her face in his hand, smoothing his thumbs across her cheeks. "My only regret is if that was Zendaris, he might be coming after you again. I don't understand why he didn't take the laptop with him."

Clasping one of his wrists, she tugged him toward the computer and pointed at the screen.

J.D. read the words in the file aloud. "The file on this laptop was a decoy. My roommate, Noelle Dupree, knows nothing about the plans or my secret life. If anything happens to me, I'll know who to blame—both Nico Zendaris and the agents of Prospero. Keep looking, but you'll never find it."

J.D. shook his head. "All this turmoil and the file isn't even on the laptop."

"That's a good thing, isn't it? He has to believe now that I know nothing about the plans."

"That's why he took off, if that was really Zendaris. Nothing left for him here."

"You had an opportunity to nail him."

"And risk your life for that?" He brushed his lips across hers. "Not worth it."

Ted groaned from the corner.

"Oh my God. I forgot all about Ted." She rushed to the fallen chair her brother was still tied to.

J.D. crouched beside her and sliced through Ted's restraints with a knife.

Blinking, Ted rubbed his wrists. "What happened?"

"I sort of knocked you out when I came through the mudroom. Good thing that floor in there was rotted clean away. Are you okay?"

"That depends. What happened to every—?" Ted broke

off, his eyes widening as they took in the mayhem of the room. "Where's the other guy?"

"He got away." J.D. grabbed Noelle's hand. "But we'll get him…one of these days."

Epilogue

Noelle joined the two spies in the Spy Museum for lunch—
it seemed so right.

And being back in D.C. seemed right, too. She'd handed
the ranch over to Ted. He'd proven himself an adult, and
she couldn't control his behavior anyway.

She placed her soup and sandwich on the table and
turned to stack the red tray on top of the others. The edge
of her tray hung over the stack, and she didn't even feel
the need to shove it into place.

J.D. hopped up to pull out her chair and kissed her
cheek. "Have a seat, darlin'. We were just talking about
you."

Her gaze meandered between J.D. and another Prospero agent from Team Three, Gage Booker. The two men
couldn't be more different, but they both possessed that
quality of being on the edge, tightly coiled and ready to
spring.

"Do you still have your suspicions of me?" She scooped
up a spoonful of soup and blew on it.

J.D.'s whiskey eyes tracked her every movement and
darkened as he zeroed in on her lips. "I never suspected
you. I was just doing my job."

Gage raised one brow. "Is that what you call it? Cade

may have been overly involved in protecting Jenna, but he had an excuse. They were already married."

"And we soon will be." J.D. ran his fingers along her arm, and the electricity she'd felt the first time he'd touched her still sizzled between them.

This time Gage raised both eyebrows. "This is news. Does Jack know?"

"Thanks for the congratulations." Noelle slurped her soup and then kissed J.D. with her warm lips.

Sliding a hand along the back of her neck, he deepened the kiss.

Gage cleared his throat. "If Jack doesn't know, I'm sure he'll find out soon enough the way you two are carrying on."

J.D. grinned and picked up his sandwich. "Jack doesn't know yet, but I'm handing the baton off to you, Gage. I understand we got some useful information out of Pia, the woman I dropped outside of the cabin."

"We sure did. We got a possible lead on one of Zendaris's houses in South America. We have to confirm a few more pieces of information before we can get the exact location and move in."

"So, you're still going after Zendaris even though nobody has the anti-drone plans?" She took a bite of the sandwich J.D. held to her lips.

Gage rolled his eyes. "We'll go after Zendaris anytime, anywhere. I'm amazed you were clear thinking enough to save that woman for questioning, what with all the other distractions going on."

"He's jealous." J.D. extended his long legs and crossed his arms behind his head. "He was always considered the ladies' man of the bunch."

"You're so full of it." Gage leveled a finger at Noelle.

"Don't get taken in by that slow Texas drawl, Noelle. But I suppose it's already too late."

"Way too late." She reached for J.D. and squeezed his hand. "It was too late for me the minute he came to my rescue in the parking lot of the grocery store."

"He did tell you he messed with that truck first so you'd need his help?"

She just squeezed tighter. "I'm so glad he did."

"Okay, you two are hopeless and kind of annoying." He pushed back from the table. "I'm going to check out the desserts and you can make goo-goo eyes at each other all you want."

"Jealous."

When Gage left the table, J.D. scooted his chair closer to hers and curled an arm around her shoulders. "I thought he'd never leave."

"He'll be coming back." She tilted her chin at Gage surveying the desserts.

"Then I guess I don't have much time."

Her heart fluttered. Did he plan on going somewhere before the wedding? After the wedding?

"Time for what?"

"Time to tell you how much I love you and can't wait to make you mine once and for all."

The heart flutters didn't subside, but now happiness instead of nerves fueled them.

"Are you ready?" She threaded her fingers through his. "Are you ready to wake up one day and find all your shirts hung up in the same direction by length and color and occasion?"

"I should be so lucky. My closet's a mess."

Her smile wavered. "I'm serious, J.D."

He kissed her lips to stop her words. "I'm serious, too, Noelle. There's no other woman in the world for me. And if you start feeling anxious?" His lids fell half-mast over his eyes and a wicked smile curved his lips. "I have ways of releasing tension you can only imagine."

She took his face in her hands and kissed him long and hard. This man could never make her feel anxious or nervous or guilty—only loved.

And love was the best medicine of all.

* * * * *

Look for more books in Carol Ericson's
BROTHERS IN ARMS: FULLY ENGAGED
miniseries later in 2013. You can find them wherever Harlequin Intrigue books are sold!

REQUEST YOUR FREE BOOKS!
2 FREE NOVELS PLUS 2 FREE GIFTS!

♦ HARLEQUIN®

INTRIGUE®

BREATHTAKING ROMANTIC SUSPENSE

YES! Please send me 2 FREE Harlequin Intrigue® novels and my 2 FREE gifts (gifts are worth about $10). After receiving them, if I don't wish to receive any more books, I can return the shipping statement marked "cancel." If I don't cancel, I will receive 6 brand-new novels every month and be billed just $4.49 per book in the U.S. or $5.24 per book in Canada. That's a savings of at least 14% off the cover price! It's quite a bargain! Shipping and handling is just 50¢ per book in the U.S. and 75¢ per book in Canada.* I understand that accepting the 2 free books and gifts places me under no obligation to buy anything. I can always return a shipment and cancel at any time. Even if I never buy another book, the two free books and gifts are mine to keep forever.

182/382 HDN FVQV

Name _____ (PLEASE PRINT)

Address _____ Apt. #

City _____ State/Prov. _____ Zip/Postal Code

Signature (if under 18, a parent or guardian must sign)

Mail to the **Harlequin® Reader Service:**
IN U.S.A.: P.O. Box 1867, Buffalo, NY 14240-1867
IN CANADA: P.O. Box 609, Fort Erie, Ontario L2A 5X3
**Are you a subscriber to Harlequin Intrigue books
and want to receive the larger-print edition?
Call 1-800-873-8635 or visit www.ReaderService.com.**

* Terms and prices subject to change without notice. Prices do not include applicable taxes. Sales tax applicable in N.Y. Canadian residents will be charged applicable taxes. Offer not valid in Quebec. This offer is limited to one order per household. Not valid for current subscribers to Harlequin Intrigue books. All orders subject to credit approval. Credit or debit balances in a customer's account(s) may be offset by any other outstanding balance owed by or to the customer. Please allow 4 to 6 weeks for delivery. Offer available while quantities last.

Your Privacy—The Harlequin® Reader Service is committed to protecting your privacy. Our Privacy Policy is available online at www.ReaderService.com or upon request from the Harlequin Reader Service.

We make a portion of our mailing list available to reputable third parties that offer products we believe may interest you. If you prefer that we not exchange your name with third parties, or if you wish to clarify or modify your communication preferences, please visit us at www.ReaderService.com/consumerschoice or write to us at Harlequin Reader Service Preference Service, P.O. Box 9062, Buffalo, NY 14269. Include your complete name and address.

HII3

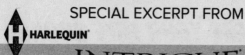
THE MARSHAL'S HOSTAGE
by USA TODAY *bestselling author*

Delores Fossen

*A sexy U.S. marshal and a feisty bride-to-be must go on
the run when danger from their past resurfaces....*

"Where the hell do you think you're going?" Dallas demanded.

But he didn't wait for an answer. He hurried to her, hauled her onto his shoulder caveman-style and carried her back into the dressing room.

That's when she saw the dark green Range Rover squeal to a stop in front of the church.

Owen.

Joelle struggled to get out of Dallas's grip, but he held on and turned to see what had captured her attention. Owen, dressed in a tux, stepped from the vehicle and walked toward his men. She had only seconds now to defuse this mess.

"I have to talk to him," she insisted.

"No. You don't," Dallas disagreed.

Joelle groaned because that was the pigheaded tone she'd encountered too many times to count.

"I'll be the one to talk to Owen," Dallas informed her. "I want to find out what's going on."

Joelle managed to slide out of his grip and put her feet on the floor. She latched on to his arm to stop him from going to the door. "You can't. You have no idea how bad things can get if you do that."

He stopped, stared at her. "Does all of this have something to do with your report to the governor?"

She blinked, but Joelle tried to let that be her only reaction. "No."

"Are you going to tell me what this is all about?" Dallas demanded.

"I can't. It's too dangerous." Joelle was ready to start begging him to leave. But she didn't have time to speak.

Dallas hooked his arm around her, lifted her and tossed her back over his shoulder.

"What are you doing?" Joelle tried to get away, tried to get back on her feet, but he held on tight.

Dallas threw open the dressing room door and started down the hall with her. "I'm kidnapping you."

Be sure to pick up
THE MARSHAL'S HOSTAGE
by USA TODAY *bestselling author Delores Fossen,*
on sale April 23 wherever
Harlequin Intrigue books are sold!